Julia turned away, a bit nonplused. . . .

Before she met the new Lord Ellston, she had thought he was probably a great prig. A dreadful high stickler. What other kind of person would break with his own father just because that father married an actress? And then to stay away for years!

Julia was not accustomed to priggish people. For that reason, she had not really looked forward to meeting him at all.

But then, he had not seemed so priggish when she met him in the lane. She had caused him to be thrown from his horse, to fall in the mud and become absolutely filthy. Any other man in his situation would have been furious. And she rather suspected he *had* been angry at first.

Then he had laughed. He had even flirted with her. He had treated the whole awful scene as a country lark. It had been almost—fun.

Until she realized who he truly was. . . .

The Errant Earl

Amanda McCabe

A SIGNET BOOK

SIGNET
Published by New American Library, a division of
Penguin Putnam Inc., 375 Hudson Street,
New York, New York 10014, U.S.A.
Penguin Books Ltd, 80 Strand,
London WC2R 0RL, England
Penguin Books Australia Ltd, Ringwood,
Victoria, Australia
Penguin Books Canada Ltd, 10 Alcorn Avenue,
Toronto, Ontario, Canada M4V 3B2
Penguin Books (N.Z.) Ltd, 182–190 Wairau Road,
Auckland 10, New Zealand

Penguin Books Ltd, Registered Offices:
Harmondsworth, Middlesex, England

First published by Signet, an imprint of New American Library,
a division of Penguin Putnam Inc.

First Printing, June 2002
10 9 8 7 6 5 4 3 2 1

To Genes, Liz, and Kells
(aka Gena Showalter, Elizabeth Branham,
and Kelli McBride)
for all your wonderful help.

Prologue

And thereby hangs a tale.

—*As You Like It*

"How *dare* you, Father? Running off to Gretna Green with some actress, of all women. And Mother scarcely cold in her grave."

"How dare *you*, Marcus! How can you speak to me, your father, in such a disrespectful manner? Have I raised a viper, who will say such things to me beneath my very roof?"

The escalating, passionate voices of the Earl of Ellston and his son floated out of the half-open door of the library and spread its poison slowly across the entire house. The dark cloud of anger crept through the marble-and-gilt foyer and up the grand staircase to the ears of the young woman who huddled there, half hidden by a carved balustrade.

Julia Barclay longed to scream, to shout, to plug up her ears, to do anything to stop the noise of the argument. But it just went on and on.

"I am twenty-one years old now, Father," Marcus, Viscount Westbrooke, said. "I am a man now, and I must protest, as a man would, these shocking actions you have taken! To bring an actress and her—her

offspring into Mother's house is unconscionable."
There was a pounding of a fist on a wooden surface,
vibrating even in the foyer, as his anger obviously
mounted.

"Barbara, God rest her soul, has been gone for over
two years. It is perfectly respectable for me to
marry again."

"To marry again, yes, if to someone like Lady Edgemere or Mrs. Barnstaple. But an actress . . ."

There was suddenly a great crash, as if some object
flew across the room, then smashed against the wall.
Julia ducked her head onto her knees and squeezed
her eyes shut.

"You will never refer to my wife in such a way
again!" roared the earl. "You will show her the respect due the Countess of Ellston."

"The Countess of Ellston is my mother," Marcus
growled. "Not some Drury Lane opera dancer."

Julia's fear instantly disappeared at his rude
words, and was replaced by indignation at the slur
to her mother. What an ignorant son her new stepfather had! Her mother was *not* an opera dancer—she
was the most acclaimed Shakespearean actress in all
of England.

Julia was so affronted by those words that she very
nearly marched down to the library to inform him
of that fact. Her stepfather's next outburst kept her
on her marble seat.

"You should be careful! You may be all of twenty-
one, but I am still your father, and I can still thrash
you."

Marcus gave a contemptuous laugh. "I should like
to see you try."

There was a long, heavy silence. Then the earl sighed, and said in a strangely quiet but firmly resolute voice, "I hate this strife between us, Marcus. But I must insist that you show my wife and her daughter respect."

Julia felt a faint prickling of tears behind her eyes at this quiet pronouncement. Tears that were somehow more frightening than the fear or the indignation had been.

She blinked furiously to keep them from falling.

Marcus's answer was a long time in coming. "And if I refuse to live by your commands?"

"Then I fear I must ask you to leave Rosemount."

"My course is clear, then. Good-bye, Father."

The library door opened completely. A tall figure emerged, closed the door behind him softly, and moved slowly across the foyer. His footsteps echoed hollowly in the vast marble space.

Julia shrank back into the shadows as he turned and looked up the staircase. She had absolutely no desire to be seen, to be drawn in any way into the quarrel. It had been quite bad enough to hear it.

Then a ray of late-afternoon sunlight came through the high windows, piercing the marble gloom and illuminating his face. She pressed a hand to her mouth to quiet her gasp.

Marcus Hadley was quite, quite beautiful. His face had the clean, austere lines of a young Renaissance saint, with dark, curling hair that brushed back from his brow and temples in an overlong fall.

But it was not his beauty that startled her so. It was the fact that his lovely eyes were filled with tears as he looked back upon his home. Julia longed to call out to him, to run down the stairs to his side and offer comfort. All she could do was sit there, numb.

Then he turned away, taking up his cloak from the chair where he had tossed it when he stormed in. The front door closed behind him, and he was gone.

He never noticed her sitting there.

The thick silence he left behind him was far worse than any shouting. The dark cloud seemed blacker than ever.

Julia leaned her forehead on her knees again. It was not supposed to be like this. When her mother had told her she was going to marry the earl, she had promised that their lives would be different now. There would be no more going out on tours, with different lodgings every month. Julia would not have to do her lessons in her mother's noisy dressing rooms. They would have a true home, a quiet, safe home that would be always theirs. Anna had been so sure when she had spoken of it, so full of love for her new husband and optimism for their future.

And Julia had caught that enthusiasm. She had always enjoyed meeting the infinite variety of people to be found in theatrical life. She had liked seeing all sorts of new cities and towns. But she was fifteen years old now; as all her mother's friends kept telling her, she would need to begin thinking of her future very soon. She was not a great beauty like her golden-haired mother. She was not a great actress like her mother. Julia drew in a deep breath and reflected that all she really wanted for her future was a nice home, a place where all of the friends she and

her mother had made over the years could visit and
where she could always return to.

It had seemed that with her mother's marriage, all
of those dreams could come true. When the three of
them had returned from Gretna Green, and Julia had
seen the glorious vision of Rosemount for the first
time, she had been sure that her dreams were real.
She had a home, and a dear man who loved her
mother and was kind to Julia.

But no sooner had their trunks been unloaded
from the carriage than the earl's son had come tear-
ing down the drive, hell-for-leather. And Julia had
known that her precious, newfound peace was soon
to be shaken.

"Darling?"

A soft hand touched Julia's shoulder, and she
looked up, startled, to find her mother bending over
her. Anna's lovely face was creased with concern.

"Darling!" she said. "You are crying."

Only then did Julia realize that her cheeks were
wet with the tears she had been trying so hard not to
shed. She wiped at them furiously with her knuckles.

"Here, Jule, dear." Anna pressed a rose-scented
handkerchief into her hand and sat down on the marble step beside her. "Tell me what is the matter."

Julia leaned against her mother's silk-covered
shoulder. Ever since her babyhood, after her father,
James Barclay, the actor, had died, she and her
mother had been their own little world of two. They
had always looked after each other. Julia never
wanted to hurt her mother, but she simply could not
keep it inside or she would burst.

"Oh, Mama!" she cried. "It was such a hideous quarrel."

Anna put her arm about Julia and hugged her close. "Between Gerald and his son?"

"Yes! They shouted so, and threw things, and then Gerald told his son to leave and not come back."

"Oh, darling, I am sorry you heard that. Why did you not stay in your new chamber, where it's quiet?"

"I just wanted some tea. So I thought I would go look for the kitchen. But then I heard the arguing, and I was scared to go any farther."

"If you wanted tea, why did you not just ring the bell? The maid would have brought you some."

Julia looked up, startled. "I-I did not think of that."

Anna laughed softly. "Oh, Jule! I told you things will be different now. I also told you that not everyone would be welcoming at first."

"Yes. You did."

Anna kissed her cheek. "My dear, you do so want to make everyone happy. But I would not worry too much about young Marcus. He will come about in time. And then we will all be one happy family."

"I hope so, Mama."

"I know so."

The earl emerged from the library then, and made his way slowly across the foyer. He seemed twenty years older than the robust, dark-haired man who had carried Anna across the threshold only that morning. He was pale and drawn in the dying light.

Then he looked up, saw them there on the staircase, and smiled. "Well, my dears," he said, obviously making a great effort to be hearty and cheerful, "what are you doing sitting about on that cold staircase?"

Anna gave him an answering smile. "We were just speculating on what your cook, whom we have heard such excellent things about, might have concocted for supper, Gerald. We are quite famished!"

"Why, what do you think?" He winked at Julia, making her giggle despite her fears. "Wedding cake, of course!"

Chapter One

Praising what is lost
Makes the remembrance dear.
                    —*All's Well That Ends Well*

Four Years Later

The village of Little Dipping was quiet on the crisp autumn afternoon when Marcus Hadley, now the Earl of Ellston, returned. Most of the local farmers were busy with bringing in the last of the harvest, leaving only a few elderly gentlemen nodding over pints in the Queen's Head, and some ladies gossiping over lace and ribbons in the shops.

Marcus was glad of the quiet. Perhaps it meant he could avoid seeing anyone he knew for just a while longer.

He left his horse at the livery stable and strolled slowly along Little Dipping's main street. So very little had changed in four years. The buildings, half-timbered, close-packed relics of another era, still blocked the sunlight, casting the cobbled walkways into shadow. The faded, painted sign of the Queen's Head, named when Anne was queen and never changed, still creaked in the breeze. He could even have sworn that the display of hats in the milliner's window was just the same as it had been when his mother shopped there.

His mother, who had now slept in the churchyard of St. Anne's for nigh on six years. And who was now joined by his father and his second wife, dead for eight months in a carriage accident.

Marcus had made his first stop at St. Anne's, where he had spoken with the vicar, Mr. Whitig, and examined the new marble memorial. Even as he had seen the names carved there, Gerald Hadley, Earl of Ellston, and Anna Hadley, Countess of Ellston, it had not seemed real.

It still felt as if his father would be waiting for him at Rosemount. That was what Marcus had been counting on during his years of wandering—that his father waited at Rosemount, and eventually they would be reconciled. All those harsh words, words Marcus now bitterly regretted, would be forgotten.

But instead, his father had died on his way to a holiday in Bath with his wife. And Marcus was left to shoulder the burden of Rosemount and the Ellston title without absolution.

Marcus paused to stare sightlessly at a shop's rather dusty window display. He knew that there were only two things he could do for his father now. He could be the finest Earl of Ellston Society had ever seen, could bring honor to the name with a good marriage and exemplary political service.

And he could see to the proper schooling and come-out of his stepmother's little child. He remembered vaguely that she had brought a small daughter to Rosemount, and he knew that the child had not been in the carriage with them on that fatal day.

He was still deep in these thoughts when the door to the shop opened and a tall matron, majestic in a purple plumed bonnet, emerged. She was closely followed by a maid, heavily laden with packages, who very nearly collided with her when she stopped abruptly.

"Marcus!" the matron cried. "Marcus Hadley, is it really you?"

Marcus turned away from the window. "Lady Edgemere! Such a surprise to see you here."

"I would vow you are not half as surprised as I!" She hurried toward him, her gloved hands outstretched. "I had no idea you were back at Rosemount."

He took her hands in his and kissed them fondly. Lady Edgemere had been one of his mother's bosom bows, and had dandled him on her knee when he was an infant. "I am not back there yet. I have only just arrived in the village and have not yet seen Rosemount."

She arched her brow. "You did not go there the very first thing?"

"No. I wished to stop at St. Anne's first."

Lady Edgemere nodded in understanding. "Oh, yes. Such a shock your dear father's passing was to us all. It was so unexpected; so very near Christmas, and the whole neighborhood thrown into mourning! Heaven only knows why he wanted to go to Bath of all places at such a time." She tilted back her head, her regard suddenly sharp. "We had expected you back much sooner, Marcus dear."

He could almost feel himself blushing for the first time in many years. He shifted on his feet. "Yes.

Well. I started out from Italy as soon as I heard the news, of course. But I was delayed several times." That was the truth, but somehow it felt like a flimsy excuse to avoid his duties.

"Hm. Well, you are here now, and that is all that matters. What are your plans, now that you are returned?"

"My plans, Lady Edgemere?"

"Yes, and I do wish you would call me Aunt Fanny, as you did when you were a child."

"I would be honored—Aunt Fanny."

"Excellent. I refer, of course, to your plans for the future. Surely you will soon be thinking of marrying."

Marcus nearly choked on that "m" word. He had so studiously avoided it for so long, but now of course there was no escape. "Of course I will. Whenever the right lady may be found."

As if summoned by the words, a young woman on horseback, very elegant in a modish green velvet habit and feathered hat, came trotting up the street. Her sleek auburn hair gleamed in the sunlight, and her carriage was erect yet easy in the saddle. She nodded to Lady Edgemere, and her eyes widened when she spied Marcus.

She gave a jaunty little wave with her crop, then turned a corner and was gone.

Lady Edgemere smiled slyly. "I am certain that finding the 'right lady' will be no trouble at all, if by right you mean of good family with a substantial dowry. You remember Lady Angela Fleming? The daughter of the Marquess of Belvoir?"

Of course Marcus remembered Lady Angela Flem-

ing. Her father's estate, Belvoir Abbey, marched with
Rosemount, and she had always tagged about after
him when they were children. And ran tattling when
he and his friends did something naughty.

She looked nothing like that spoiled child now.

"I remember Lady Angela," he said.

"And I am certain she remembers *you*."

Marcus laughed. "I am not quite ready for the par-
son's mousetrap yet, Aunt Fanny."

"Then what do you intend to do in the
meantime?"

"Well, for one thing I must see to my father's
wife's little child."

Lady Edgemere gave him a most odd look indeed.
"Her little child?"

"Yes. She had a daughter, did she not? No doubt
the tot is running quite wild at Rosemount, with only
her nanny or nursemaid or whatever. I was . . . less
than kind to my stepmother," he admitted ruefully.
"I want to make some amends now, by sending the
child to a proper school. Perhaps giving her a Season
one day."

Lady Edgemere's faded blue eyes took on a suspicious new sparkle. "Well, I must tell you that Anna
and I became great friends; she turned out to be not
quite what we all expected. I can only hope that her
daughter will do the same for you."

Before Marcus could question her about this odd
statement, she kissed his cheek and said, "I must be
running along now, Marcus dear. But I hope that you
will come to supper at Edgemere Park very soon."

Marcus watched her walk away, then turned

toward the livery where he had left his horse. It was time for him to return to Rosemount at last. He wondered what he would find when he got there.

Julia sat on one of the wide window seats in the morning room at Rosemount, her knees drawn up beneath her chin as she watched the rehearsal taking place before her.

Not long after the death of her mother and stepfather, Anna's old friends Abelard Douglas and his Troupe of Ambling Players had landed on the doorstep of Rosemount. They had come in search of shelter, a safe haven where they could rest and rehearse for their next tour of Shakespeare's comedies.

Julia, lonely and deep in misery, had welcomed her "Uncle Abby," just as her mother had always welcomed any friends. Julia delighted in the company of the merry players, and the morning room had been turned into an impromptu theater, with a roughly built stage at one end. It became the scene of many wild romps and farces, much to the oft-expressed horror of the staid butler and his equally staid wife, the housekeeper.

In only a few months, the actors' antics had taken over the silent corridors of Rosemount, and Julia had even begun to laugh again, when she had thought the loss of her mother and Gerald had robbed the world of any merriment. They involved her in their rehearsals, their plans, and their quarrels, where before all she could do was brood.

They had saved her life.

And now here they were, only a little more than a month away from beginning their grand tour, rehearsing their latest play, *As You Like It*. It had been Anna's favorite play, and was Julia's, too. She watched the rehearsal with delight now, the book open on her lap so she could act as prompter, and also read the lines of Rosalind, in the absence of the actress who was to play her.

Charlie Englehardt, the well-known comedian who was playing Touchstone, the clown, stomped across the stage, crying, " 'If thou beest not damned for this, the devil himself will have no shepherds; I cannot see else how thou shouldst 'scape.' "

A young apprentice actor said, " 'Here comes young Master Ganymede.' "

Then—silence.

Everyone turned to look at Julia.

"Oh!" she gasped. "Is it my turn?" As usual, she had been too enthralled by the performance to remember to read along.

"Aye, lassie," boomed Abelard, who always spoke very loudly. "Just as it was yesterday on 'Here comes young Master Ganymede.' "

Mary, the pretty blond actress playing Celia, giggled.

"Oh." Julia flipped through the pages and located her speech. " 'From the East to Western Ind, no jewel is like Rosalind. Her worth, being . . .' "

She was just beginning to enjoy herself when a disapproving cough in the doorway caught her attention.

She peeked over the top of the book to see Thompson, the butler, surveying her and all the actors down his rather short, rabbitlike nose. She wondered what she had done to upset his notions of order now.

"Yes, Thompson?" she said quietly.

"I beg your pardon, Miss Barclay," answered Thompson, peering askance at Charlie in his red, green, and yellow motley costume. Despite the fact that the actors had been at Rosemount for months, Thompson always appeared shocked when he encountered them. "It is very nearly time for tea. Cook would like to know how many will be partaking *this* time."

"Well, I am not certain," Julia began slowly. "Perhaps . . . ten?"

"John and Ned have gone off to the village," Mary offered. "But I will be there, and so will Daphne."

"So will I," boomed Abelard. "So be certain there are enough of those cream cakes this time. Yesterday, Charlie, here, ate them all, and there were none left for anyone else. We had to make do with bread and butter."

Charlie shook his circlet of bells indignantly. "Slander! Falsehoods! I did no such thing! 'Twas young Ned, or may I never tread a board again."

Mary giggled.

Thompson gave one last disapproving sniff and departed, no doubt to tell his wife all about Miss Barclay's guests' latest oddities.

"Well, I am off to change my frock," said Mary, pushing her golden curls back from her pretty face. She linked arms with Charlie and the apprentice, and the three of them ambled amiably from the room.

Julia sighed and tucked the book away in the pocket of her apron.

"Here now, lass," said Abelard, settling his considerable girth beside her on the window seat. "What was that sigh for? Is old blue-nosed Thompson making you unhappy? Just say the word, and Ned, Charlie, and I will fling him on his skinny arse into the trout stream."

Julia laughed at the vision of the butler covered in green, dripping water, with a flopping trout on his head. "Oh, Uncle Abby! No, of course it is not Thompson. I am used to him by now."

"Then what is it? You can tell your old Uncle Abby."

Julia shrugged. "I do not know. It is just that, well, these last few months of having you all here have been so grand. I can't bear to think how gloomy Rosemount will be when you are gone." And when Gerald's son came home and she had to face her future, as she had been dreading for months.

Abelard patted her hand comfortingly. "Ach, now, lass. You needn't worry about that. You're stuck with us for another month at least. We don't open in Brighton until then, y'know, and we have no money for lodgings anywhere else!"

Julia laughed. "True! We do have another month."

"You know you can always come with us when we leave. Agnes's broken foot won't heal for quite a while yet, and we'll be needing a Rosalind."

"Abby," Julia said, responding to this oft-repeated offer, "I am not the actress my mother was. . . ."

"No one is the actress your mother was," Abelard said solemnly. "Anna Barclay's Rosalind was a legend, and it was a black day when she left the stage to marry. But you are a fine actress, lass. Much better than you give yourself credit for."

"And the Barclay name on your playbill would do wonders for your receipts," she teased.

Abelard tapped his chin consideringly. "There *is* that. But truly, lass, if ever you're in need, you come to us, and we'll see you safe. Just as you have for us."

"Abby, you are a dear." Julia kissed his ginger-whiskered cheek. "I will remember that."

"Yes, well, humph. I had best be going in to tea, to get my cream cakes before that Charlie can. Are you coming, Jule? You need to eat, you know; keep your strength up. You have become so thin this last year."

"You go ahead. I promised one of the tenants, who is ill, that I would bring her some beef tea for her supper. I'll just take it to her now."

"You'll be back before dark, though?"

"Abby! It is hours until dark. I will take the main road, even though it is a bit muddy from yesterday's rain. What possible harm could befall me there?"

Chapter Two

A fool, a fool! I met a fool i' the forest.
—*As You Like It*

Marcus, having exhausted the charms of Little Dipping and being faced with the waning of the sun, was at last forced to turn his steps toward Rosemount. It was a prospect he faced with more than a little trepidation.

He was eager to see his home again. In all his years of wandering, of life in rented lodgings, inns, and hotels, he had thought so often of Rosemount. He had seen the house—gleaming dove-gray stone atop a great grassy knoll—in his mind every night before he went to sleep. It seemed in his memory a haven of peace and tranquillity. A place where everything always remained the same.

But he knew that the Rosemount he was returning to now was quite unlikely to be the serene enclave of his memory. He had been gone for years; Rosemount was no doubt changed beyond recognition. There was no telling what changes his father's wife, the *actress*, had wrought. Red velvet wallpaper? Gold tassels on all the window draperies? Chairs in the shape of dragons?

Marcus almost laughed at the outlandish visions

his mind had conjured, until he remembered how serious this all truly was.

Rosemount had been a bit shabby when Marcus's mother, Barbara, had married his father and become its mistress, or so he had often heard. His grandmother had been more concerned with gaming and running with the fast Devonshire House crowd than she had been with country houses. This had left Rosemount in a rather sorry state, when it had once been a grand showplace. Barbara had made it grand once more, and her style, light and airy as cream and sunshine, had been imitated far and wide in the *ton*.

As amusing as the thought of tables made from elephants' feet was to Marcus, he knew that he could not bear to see his mother's graceful rooms ruined by vulgarity.

At the very least, a grubby child would be toddling about along the Aubusson rugs, leaving sticky handprints on satin upholstery.

Marcus sighed, and drew his horse up at a crossroads. In one direction lay Rosemount. In the other was Belvoir Abbey, the home of Lady Angela Fleming.

For one wild moment, even going off to pay a call on Lady Angela and her father seemed preferable to going to Rosemount. Perhaps then he could arrive home long after everyone there was asleep.

But he knew that he could not do that. He had stayed away for far too long already; it was time for him to take up his responsibilities. So Marcus turned down the road toward Rosemount, spurring his horse on to a run. It was best to get the homecoming over quickly.

The lane was deserted at that time of day, the noise of his horse's hooves on the rather muddy road the only sound. The breeze that rushed past him was cool but not yet cold, carrying the crisp scents of an autumn country day.

Marcus laughed aloud at the exhilaration of it all, his trepidations and gloomy forebodings forgotten. There was truly nothing like a brisk ride in the English autumn countryside, he thought. Nothing he had seen in all his travels, not the canals of Venice, not the Alps, not even the pyramids of Egypt could compare.

God, but he had missed it.

So caught up in the thrill of the wild ride was Marcus, that he did not see the figure seated beside the lane on a low, flat boulder.

He did not see her, that is, until he was nearly atop her. Even then, she looked so much like an ethereal vision, a fairy, that he was not sure she was real. Until she leaped up from her seat with a small but piercing shriek.

"Hold, Beelzebub!" Marcus shouted to his horse, pulling back hard on the reins. "Hold!"

The horse, not at all happy with this abrupt end to his merry gallop, reared up on his hind legs, spraying the girl with mud.

And sending Marcus tumbling from the saddle to land on his backside in the very same mud. The oozing brown mess fell in a great shower over his riding coat, his face and hair. Thus relieved of his burden, Beelzebub shook his head, snorted, and trotted off to investigate an interesting clump of grass.

Marcus lay there in the lane, staring up at the sky,

utterly stunned. He wasn't certain he could even breathe. He tried to draw an experimental breath, but his ribs ached too much, so he gave up the effort and just lay there.

Then a face swam into view above him, blocking the sky and the treetops.

An angel's face. Surely such a piddling fall could not have killed him? And why would heaven look so much like the English countryside? Yet here was an angel, with a wealth of light brown curls tied back carelessly with a ribbon framing a creamy white face. Her wide hazel eyes were frightened as she looked down at him.

Then his angel shrieked. Directly into his ear.

"Oh, no, I've killed him!" she cried.

Marcus winced. "Alas, no, madam," he managed to take in enough breath to say. "I am sorry to disoblige you, but I fear I am not quite dead yet."

She startled visibly to hear him speak. "Thank the stars! I was certain you had broken your neck. I am so very sorry!"

"*You* are sorry?" Marcus would have laughed, if he hadn't been sure it would prove painful. "I nearly ran you down, and *you* are sorry?"

"I should not have been sitting there, too near the road. I was reading, you see, and did not even hear you coming."

"I should not have been going along at such a pace. I was deep in my own thoughts and not paying proper attention. So *I* am sorry."

She smiled then, and Marcus saw that she had the most delightful dimple in her right cheek. She also had the faintest smattering of pale gold freckles across her little, upturned nose.

"Well, then," she said, "since we are both properly sorry, may I help you to stand?"

"Will I not be too heavy for you?" he asked. She did not seem much bigger than a child, with slim shoulders and small hands. But the idea of having an excuse to actually touch his angel was very tempting indeed.

"Oh, no. I am stronger than I look. No doubt between us we shall have you back on your feet in a trice. Unless something is broken. Then I shall have to fetch Dr. Carter."

Marcus carefully tested his limbs. "Battered, perhaps, but not broken."

"Excellent! Then, if you can just sit up, thus, and put your arm around my shoulder, I will help you to your feet."

He did just as she instructed, and found himself leaning against her heavily as he hauled himself upright, his face very close to hers. Her hair was soft where a loose strand brushed against his cheek, and she smelled intoxicatingly of French lavender and sunshine. She did feel rather frail to him, but, true to her word, she was stronger than she looked, and he was standing upright in no time at all.

But he was loath to move away from her. He gazed down at her, quite unable to look away.

She was frowning in thought, unaware of his regard. "Do you think you could ride?" she said. "I am not certain I could help you mount."

"Hm?" Marcus murmured, her words conjuring

up images in his mind that were quite different from her true meaning.

Good gad! The fall must have addled his brain. Here he was on the very verge of his homecoming, when all his thoughts should be on the duties of the earldom he was about to take up. And instead he was having erotic daydreams about a strange girl he had nearly run down with his horse!

It was lunacy.

Obviously the girl agreed. She was looking up at him with a distinctly puzzled air.

"Your horse," she repeated rather loudly, as if she were speaking to a half-wit. "Can you ride your horse?"

"Perhaps I should just sit down on that rock for a bit," he answered. "Then I am sure I will be able to continue on my way. I can go back to the Queen's Head to get cleaned up."

"What a good idea. Here, let me move these so that there is room for you to sit." She scooped up a shawl, an empty basket, and a slim, leather-bound book, which she had dropped when leaping and shrieking. Then she helped him to sit down, and moved away to rearrange the shawl over her shoulders.

"Do you have far to travel?" she asked, leaning back idly against a tree trunk.

"Not very far," Marcus answered distractedly. She really was quite pretty, this angel of the road. Even her rather ugly dark gray dress, now flecked with mud, could not disguise that. But who was she? Some maidservant or shopkeeper's daughter? She was not at all familiar to him. "And what about you? Do you live nearby?"

"Not very far," she imitated. "I had just stopped here for a while on my way home, to read quietly."

"It isn't very quiet at your home?"

She gave a small, unladylike snort. "Scarcely! Especially not at the moment. It is quite crowded there, you see."

Surely, then, she was some shopkeeper's daughter, living above the shop with her parents and ten brothers and sisters. But she was a shopkeeper's daughter with a penchant for Shakespeare, he saw, as he tilted his head to read the gold-lettered spine of her book. Never had much use for the old Bard, himself.

"And here I came bungling along and disturbed your solitude," he said. "I am sorry."

She grinned at him. "Oh, I don't think I mind so very much."

Julia leaned back against the tree, studying from beneath her lashes the stranger she had just met so dramatically. He was really quite handsome, even covered with mud from his hair to his boots. She was sure his hair must be dark, and very curly, even though he had cropped it short in an obvious effort to subdue it. The eyes that looked out at her from the heavily dirty but fine-boned face were a celestial blue.

She thought that once he was cleaned up he would surely be more handsome even than Ned Dennis, the Ambling Player's resident Apollo. Maybe even more handsome than Mr. Elliott, the new curate.

She wondered idly who he was. His boots and

clothes were obviously expensive, as was his horse, the aptly named Beelzebub. Probably he was a guest at Belvoir Abbey.

Maybe even a suitor of the silly Lady Angela.

Julia frowned at that thought, suddenly sorry she had blurted out that she was *not* sorry he had come along.

But he was smiling at her. He took out a handkerchief and began scrubbing away at some of the thick mud on his face. "Well," he said, "I am glad you aren't sorry we met, because I am *certainly* not sorry."

Julia couldn't help but laugh. "Oh, you aren't, are you?" Was he *flirting* with her?

"No. You see, I know so few people in the neighborhood anymore. . . ."

He went on speaking, but she no longer heard him. Instead, she stood there frozen, watching in horror as he made progress in cleaning off his face. Slowly, his features were emerging from the mask of mud. Features that were even more handsome than she had speculated.

Features that were familiar.

She had seen that face only once before, four years ago, and only for an instant. It had changed, becoming thinner and sun browned. But she knew who he was.

It was her stepfather's prodigal son.

Gerald had almost never spoken of his son, except when a rare letter arrived from Marcus and he would read portions of it aloud. Gerald had tried to make their lives as happy and normal as possible, despite the breach with his son. Yet sometimes a shadow would pass over his face when he thought no one was looking, and Julia would know he was thinking of his faraway son.

It was the face she had been expecting to see every

day these last eight months, since the carriage accident. The new Earl of Ellston, come to take his place at Rosemount and toss her out of it.

Here he was at last. The future she had not wanted to face was right before her.

Marcus smiled at her now, even flirted with her a bit, while he did not know who she was. What would he say when he learned she was the daughter of the "vulgar opera dancer"?

What would he do when he saw the theater she had made of his morning room, and all the "vulgar" actors staying in his guest rooms and eating his food?

Oh, dear heaven! Abelard and the others. Their tour did not begin for another month yet, and Julia knew they did not have enough money to find lodgings for all of them. What would happen to them when this new earl tossed them out to starve in the hedgerows?

She must have gasped aloud, because he was looking at her rather oddly.

"Are you quite all right?" he asked. "You look pale. Are you certain you were not injured?"

"I—no," Julia managed to squeak. "I just—that is to say, I have to be going!"

Then she spun about and fled, running off across a field, unmindful of the mud sucking at her half boots and the hem of her skirt. He was calling after her, but she ignored him. She climbed over a low wall and slid down an embankment, out of sight of the road. Soon his voice faded completely behind her.

She ran across fields and meadows, one hand pressed to the stitch in her side.

She *had* to reach Rosemount, and quickly. Before the new earl did.

Chapter Three

A good plot, good friends, and full of ex-
pectation; an excellent plot, very good
friends.

—*Henry IV, Part One*

Julia kept running until she reached the edge of Rosemount's manicured gardens, and stopped only
when she nearly tripped on an untied lace on her
half boot.

With a low, muttered curse, she plumped herself
down on a marble bench just at the edge of the garden, and bent to retie her lace. Then she just sat there,
trying to catch her breath and gather her scattered
thoughts.

So, he was returned at last, come to claim what
was his, now that his father and the "vulgar actress"
were gone. Julia had always known, in the back of
her mind, that this day would come. Really, she was
quite fortunate it had not come much sooner.

But, in her most secret heart, she had hoped that
perhaps it would never come to pass, that something
would happen to Marcus which would make him
overlook her presence here. Not that she wished him
a violent end, or anything like that. Only that somehow he would never return. That she could go on as
she had done, safe at Rosemount.

Her home, as she had thought it to be.

Julia turned to look at the house in the distance, glistening in the rosy glow of the late sun. Rosemount had been the first secure, permanent home she had ever known, and she had found only love and peace in its walls. Her stepfather had often teased about her affection for the house, saying that once she was married and ensconced in a far grander place, she would think Rosemount a mere forester's hut. Julia had always protested; she knew that there could be no finer house in all England.

Now she would surely have to leave it, because the new earl would not want some actress's daughter hanging about. He would soon bring a wife here, a new mistress for Rosemount. Julia would have to face that uncertain future she had tried to hide from.

Perhaps she *would* join Abelard and the others on their tour, after all. . . .

Abelard and the others!

Julia covered her mouth with her hand in utter dismay. How could she possibly have forgotten them, even for a moment? She was not the only one who would be set adrift by the earl. They had no place to go until their tour began. They definitely did not have enough money to lodge and feed themselves. Julia's own inheritance of her dowry, money Gerald had set aside for her, which she was so counting on, had not yet come to her.

Her friends were in even greater danger than she was herself. The earl would surely be wary of unflattering gossip that might ensue if he tossed his father's stepdaughter out so quickly. He would have no such compunction about a group of actors.

If only she could keep them with her, for just a short while longer. Surely she could buy them a month. Then she could leave with them on their tour, or buy a little cottage with her money, and all would be well. If only there were a way . . .

Her gaze fell on the book she had dropped into her basket. She picked it up, turning the smooth leather of the cover over in her hand.

Of course. Yes. When life became difficult for Shakespeare's Rosalind and Celia, they had not fallen down and surrendered. They had forged ahead and made a new life for themselves. In disguise.

Before Julia could even go to her friends and try to form a plan with them, Thompson, the rabbity, disapproving butler, stopped her in the corridor.

"Miss Barclay," he said in his high-pitched tone, "I must give you my resignation, and that of my wife."

Julia stared at him. She knew that she should feel dismay that the butler and housekeeper were leaving, but really all she felt was profound relief. Her mother had kept the Thompsons on for so long, despite their disapproving attitudes, because she had been too tender-hearted to let them go. And they had obviously never left because the Rosemount positions were so comfortable.

Julia shared her mother's tender heart; she also was too busy to look for replacement staff.

But now, the thought of not having to face Thompson's disapproving, twitching face anymore brightened her day considerably, even in the face of Lord Ellston's approach.

Lord Ellston's approach! She was going to have to

get rid of Thompson quickly, unless she wanted a scene when the earl arrived.

She arranged her face into suitably serious lines. "I am very sorry to hear that, Thompson," she said.

"We simply cannot tolerate the circumstances any longer!" Thompson answered, still twitching. "A household should have order, a schedule. Houseguests should never stay for months! Champagne should not be drunk in the afternoon!"

His voice rose steadily, and he showed every sign of going on like this for hours.

Julia cut him off, saying, "Quite right. You would not want to compromise your ideas of order. If you or your wife will come to my book room, I will pay you the wages owed you, and you can be on your way quickly, as I am sure you wish."

Thompson nodded jerkily, turned on his heel, and stalked away.

As Julia watched him go, a new, wonderful, and, if she said so herself, brilliant idea began to take shape in her mind.

"You want me to do *what*?" Abelard boomed. "Are you daft, lass?"

Julia planted her fists on her hips and surveyed the company before her. Fortunately, they had still been gathered for tea when she finished dealing with Thompson, and she would not have to explain her plan more than once.

"I am not daft, Uncle Abby," she said stoutly. "I think it is a fine idea, especially since I came up with it on such short notice. I am sure it will work."

Actually, she was not sure of any such thing. All she knew was that they had to give it a try.

"You want me to be a butler," Abelard protested. "A servant."

Mary, whose mischievously pretty face lit up as Julia outlined her plan, said, "Nonsense, Abby! Julia is not asking you to be a servant. She is asking you to play the role of a servant."

"Exactly!" Julia cried. "Mary is right. It is merely a role. Did you not play Malvolio in *Twelfth Night*? And was he not a servant?"

Abelard rubbed at his ginger-colored whiskers doubtfully as he looked from Julia to Mary. Mary nodded encouragingly. Then he said, "You want me to play Malvolio?"

"Well, not *exactly* Malvolio," Julia answered carefully. She had the sudden sense that it was very important she nip any of her friend's more flamboyant tendencies in the bud. Before things got terribly out of control. "You need not wear yellow stockings! It is more like . . . Imagine this is a new play. With a modern setting. And you are playing the butler to an earl, and you can save the day in the last act."

Abelard brightened a bit. "And reunite the lovers?"

Yes, it was definitely time to nip things in the bud. "If there *were* lovers, I suppose you could do that." Oh, he just *had* to agree to play the butler. All the others would follow his example. It was a grand plan, and with the departure of the Thompsons, it seemed fated.

But it all depended on Abelard.

"It sounds like great fun," said Mary. "What is my role to be?"

"We think it jolly fun, too!" John and Ned, who had been mock–sword fighting in the corner, chorused. The two handsome young actors were Mary's devoted swains in all things.

"What are we to do?" asked Ned, looking to Mary for approval.

Mary tossed her golden curls, and ignored him.

Julia brought out the hasty list she had made after Thompson gave his resignation. "Mary, you and Daphne will be housemaids."

Daphne, a redheaded ingenue, giggled. "Can I be a French maid? I've been practicing, you see. *Oh la la, comme ca va la chien du vert, monsieur.*"

Julia sighed impatiently. "Daphne, dear, you can be whatever you like. But you may want to study the French language a bit more before you attempt it; what you just said makes no sense. Now, Ned and John, you will be footmen. I am afraid we have no spare livery, but perhaps some of your costumes will work."

Charlie, the clown, leaped up and down. "What about me, what about me?"

"You, Charlie, can be the cook's assistant," said Julia.

Abelard, who had begun to be infected by his troupe's obvious enthusiasm for the masquerade, still looked doubtful. "How will we learn to play our roles properly, Jule?"

"The servants will help you," Julia replied. She had already spoken to the cook, very briefly, and

Mrs. Gilbert had promised to talk to the others. All of them, with the exception of the sour Thompsons, had adored Julia's mother. They would do anything to help the friends of their "Countess Anna," as they had called her.

Even at the risk of losing their positions.

So now Julia had not only herself and the actors to worry about; she also had the servants. But she could not think of that now. There was simply too much to do in too short a time. The earl may have gone back to Little Dipping to clean up, but that would not take him all night.

She clapped her hands to recapture everyone's attention. "Now, we must hurry! I am sure Lord Ellston will be here at any moment. All of you go to the kitchen, and the servants will help you. I must go upstairs myself, and wash and change."

Julia watched them all crowding out of the drawing room, talking and laughing excitedly. Obviously, they all saw it as a great lark, a challenge to their acting talents. "Jolly fun," as Ned had said.

But Julia's heart was frozen in fear. Oh, what was she doing? The new earl would see through this ruse immediately. The man she had met in the lane was no fool. His sky blue eyes had been clear and sharp, despite their wondrous beauty.

There was no time for what-ifs now, though, or to moon over handsome eyes. This was not much of a plan, to be sure, yet it was all she could devise on such short notice. She *had* to do this, to protect them all.

Julia smoothed back her hair, squared her shoulders, and went upstairs to make herself presentable to greet the new earl.

Chapter Four

All the world's a stage.

—As You Like It

Marcus drew up his horse at the crest of a hill to look down on Rosemount.

It looked exactly the same as it had when he had left. Solid, substantial, but still indescribably beautiful. Especially with its pale gray stone surrounded by the gold and amber of autumn leaves, the rosy glow of the setting sun. It was all a burst of color, as if gaily bedecked to welcome him home.

Marcus laughed aloud at his fanciful thoughts. The meeting with the Shakespearean fairy girl in the lane had obviously had an effect on him. He was so very seldom fanciful.

As he turned his horse onto the long, curving drive, he wondered again who the girl was. While bathing and changing his clothes at the Queen's Head, he had begun to think that she must be the daughter of a gentleman farmer rather than a shopkeeper, someone prosperous. Her fair skin and soft hands had not spoken of someone who had to work. But he could not think of anyone in the neighborhood who would have a daughter of the right age.

Then again, he had been gone for a long time. People had surely moved in and out of the neighborhood, and there would be some who were strangers to him. Perhaps he would soon encounter her again; perhaps he would not.

He certainly hoped that he would.

He shook his head to try to free it of his obsessive thoughts of the mystery girl. There were too many responsibilities he had to consider just then. He could not afford to be preoccupied with an angel when his homecoming was imminent.

Later, perhaps.

As he neared the house, he noticed the neat garden beds, the last of the flowers just beginning to fade. The two fountains were running, sending streams of sparkling water into the air and spilling it down their marble sides, filling the air with the tinkling aquamarine music. The two statues alongside the front steps, of Athena and Demeter, still gleamed white in the dying light. It was all as he remembered it, every detail. Nothing had changed.

That is, until the butler threw open the front door at his approach.

The butler whom Marcus remembered, a man named Timothy, or perhaps Thompkins, who had only been at Rosemount for a brief while before he left, had been a small, rabbitlike man with a perpetual air of disapproval. This man, on the other hand, was large, a veritable giant, with a wild mane of red hair and a tangle of ginger whiskers. His wide shoulders strained at his black coat, and he wore a most unbutlerlike waistcoat of purple-and-gold satin stripes.

"Lord Ellston, I presume?" he boomed, his loud voice resonating in the cool evening air.

"Er . . . yes," Marcus answered slowly. He handed his horse's reins to the waiting groom and went up the shallow marble front steps to where the butler waited. "And you are? . . ."

"Douglas, my lord."

"Oh. A Scot?"

The butler gave a very elaborate bow. "You have an acute ear, my lord."

It was difficult to miss the burr when the man was shouting it right in Marcus's ear. He nodded and looked past Douglas's massive shoulder to see two housemaids, a tall redhead and a little, curly haired blonde, standing by the grand staircase. They were respectably attired in black dresses and crisp white aprons and caps, but they were eyeing him rather boldly and whispering behind their hands.

Marcus frowned. He had not expected that everything would remain just the same in his absence. Yet he had not thought that his father's wife might fill the house with eccentric servants.

He glanced around the foyer, half suspecting that it might now be painted purple or have naughty frescoes on the walls. But it was the same. The same old family portraits looking down on him from cream silk-papered walls. The same carved round Jacobean table and gold velvet-upholstered chairs lined the walls outside the closed library and drawing room doors. The same soaring ceiling. The only change was that the cold marble floor was now covered by a rug in glowing shades of crimson and blue.

Marcus looked up into the shadows at the top of

the staircase, wondering what else was the same in his home, and what had changed.

"Would you care to come into the drawing room, my lord?" Douglas boomed, startling Marcus out of his reverie. "Refreshments have been ordered, and Miss Barclay will be with you very shortly."

"Miss Barclay?" Marcus said, puzzled. "Is it not rather late for her?"

Douglas's bushy red brows knit together. "Late, my lord? It is not even seven o'clock. Perhaps that is late where you came from?" He looked as if Marcus had only lately arrived from the moon and could have no idea about the proper way of doing things.

"No, it is not." But surely it was late for a child? Marcus had little experience with children. Perhaps the little beasts stayed up until dawn. "Well, then, I suppose her nursemaid could bring her down for a while."

Douglas's brows shot up. "Her nursemaid, my lord?"

Was the child too old for a nursemaid? Maybe she had a governess now. He couldn't puzzle it out just then; he was aching for a brandy and something to eat. It had been such a decidedly odd day. "Just have her come down when she is ready, then, Douglas," he said, and went into the drawing room.

Douglas smiled hugely. "Oh, *yes*, my lord."

After Julia had changed her dress and tidied her hair as best she could, she went into the guest chamber next door to her own. Agnes, the leading lady of Abelard's Ambling Players, had been laid up there ever since she had broken her foot falling off the stage.

"Do I look presentable?" Julia asked, smoothing the skirt of her lavender gown. "Or shall I be a disgrace?"

Agnes looked up from the costume she was mending. "You look very pretty, Julia! What is the occasion? A party?"

Julia gave a little snort. "Not a party! I still tell everyone I am in mourning. And now that Mother and Gerald are gone, that Lady Angela Fleming will surely have her way at last, and I will be outcast, with no invitations at all." She fell into a mock-despairing swoon across a chaise. "Alas, alas! Never to attend a musicale at the Hallsbys' again! Never to have Freddie Barnstaple trod on my toes at a ball again! Whatever shall I do?"

Agnes laughed. "A cruel fate, indeed. But I would not get my hopes up if I were you. No one will listen to that spoiled Lady Angela, and you will have to go out in company very soon."

Julia shook her head. "Lady Angela Fleming is the reigning Beauty of the neighborhood, and she has hated me ever since I tripped and spilled punch on her at my first ball. But I have greater worries than that tonight."

"Really? What has happened?"

"The new earl is arrived."

"No!" Agnes gasped. "Have you met him? What is he like?"

"I did meet him this afternoon, but he did not know it was me." Julia then proceeded to outline the whole ridiculous scene in the muddy lane.

Agnes fell back against her pillows in helpless laughter. "Oh, Julia! I would so dearly love to see his face when he realizes who you are."

Julia grimaced. "Perhaps you could go down instead of me? You are so pretty; you would make a much better me than I do."

"Oh, no. You are the leading lady of this farce. But you must tell me all about it after. I am planning on writing my own play, you know; I always need fresh material."

Julia sighed. "Yes, I'll tell you all."

Agnes glanced ruefully around her comfortable room, with its cozy fire in the grate and its clutter of scripts and costumes. "I suppose our days in this warm little nest are numbered."

"What?"

"Well, now that his lordship is here, I am sure he will not want a ragtag group of players cluttering up his corridors. We will have to leave."

"The doctor said you are not to be moved until your foot heals!"

"Nevertheless . . ."

Julia shook her head. "You needn't worry about that, Agnes, at least for a while. I have a scheme."

Agnes's dark eyes glowed. "Oh, I do adore a *scheme*! Tell me what it is."

"It all began when Thompson gave his notice."

"That rabbity butler?"

"Yes. So we need a butler, and you all need a place to stay. Abelard will be the butler, and everyone else will be various members of the staff."

Agnes clapped her hands in delight. "Our greatest

theatrical challenge yet! Superb. What is my role to be?"

"You can be my cousin, unfortunately taken ill."

"Oh, excellent! Then I can see that you are properly chaperoned." Agnes pursed her lips sternly.

Julia laughed at her unconvincing prim-and-proper air. "I must go meet his lordship now. I cannot delay the inevitable forever. I only wanted to tell you what the scheme is."

"I am very glad you did. I vow I have not been so diverted in weeks!"

Marcus sipped at his brandy and studied the portrait displayed over the fireplace in the vast rose-and-gold drawing room. It was of an extraordinarily beautiful woman, with long golden hair falling over the shoulders of her blue velvet, Italian Renaissance–style gown. One slender hand rested on an iron box. Hazel eyes seemed to laugh down at him, dancing with gold and green lights. The brass plate affixed to the frame read, MRS. ANNA BARCLAY, AS PORTIA IN *THE MERCHANT OF VENICE*."

Shakespeare again.

"Lord Ellston?" a soft voice said behind him.

Marcus turned and found a pair of hazel eyes exactly like the ones in the portrait regarding him steadily. Yet this time they came from the face of his angel of the lane.

She had changed her ugly gray frock for one of dusky lavender muslin with a small standing ruff of silvery lace that framed her face prettily. Her wild curls were now neatly brushed and pulled back into a knot at the nape of her neck. But it was undoubtedly her. What the deuce was she doing *here,* in his very own house?

He could not say a word. Indeed, he could only look at her with what he feared was a rather stupid expression on his face.

Her chin trembled just a bit, but she smiled bravely and stepped closer to him, her hand outstretched. "I fear we had not the chance for proper introductions earlier," she said quietly. "I am Julia Barclay."

Marcus was stunned. *She* was Julia Barclay? Anna Barclay's daughter? How could that be? Julia Barclay was a child, and his angel was . . .

Obviously not a child.

All of his foolish assumptions crumpled into dust, and he knew that now he would be forced to reevaluate his plans. Drastically. A grown woman was an entirely different kettle of fish than a child. Far more complicated.

An attractive grown woman was even worse.

However, he could not solve those difficulties at that very moment. Julia Barclay—the *real* Julia Barclay—was standing before him with her hand held out to him.

He took that hand and bowed over it politely. Her skin was rather chilled, and her hand shook slightly in his grasp, as if she were a bit nervous. But her faint, polite smile was still in place.

"Things *were* rather chaotic at the time of our meeting," he answered. "It was rather too bad of you not to tell me who you were, though, Miss Barclay."

Her smiled wavered. She withdrew her hand from his grasp and settled herself on a small chair drawn up beside the fire. "If you will recall, Lord Ellston, things were quite confusing. What with the mud, and your horse, and my thinking you had been killed, and such. And I had no idea who you were. Then."

Marcus seated himself across from her, still rather bemused by the turn of events. "I had imagined that you were a small child, Miss Barclay."

She raised her brow delicately. "Did you, indeed? How extraordinary."

They studied each other warily in the awkward silence that fell between them. It was only interrupted when the giggling housemaids Marcus had seen earlier came in bearing a tray of refreshments.

They arranged the food clumsily on a low table next to Julia, nearly knocking over a pot of tea in the process. One of them, he could have sworn, *winked* at Julia as they curtsied and left the room.

What a very curious household. He would have to have a long discussion with the housekeeper about the staff.

But tomorrow. Not tonight. Tonight, he was rather tired, and it was very pleasant to be in the company of a pretty lady, even if she *was* Julia Barclay.

In the firelight, Anna Barclay's daughter was very pretty indeed. Her white hands were deft as they poured out two cups of tea and arranged sandwiches and cakes on a plate. He could faintly smell her lavender scent, and she was humming some soft tune beneath her breath.

The two of them seemed an island of warmth and

golden light in the vast darkness of the drawing room. In the silence, the old house seemed to slumber around them.

It was all so peaceful, Rosemount, his home. The home he had so foolishly run from, stayed away from. It wrapped itself around him, welcoming him back.

He could have wept. Indeed, he feared he might have if a gentle voice had not broken into his maudlin reverie.

"Would you care for some tea, Lord Ellston?" Julia said.

Marcus looked up to find her hazel eyes watching him over the thin rim of a china teacup. She smiled softly, understandingly, almost as if she had divined his thoughts.

Then he became too acutely aware that she was *not* just a pretty woman to sit peacefully by the fire with. She was the actress's daughter. It would be wrong for him to be vulnerable before her.

His jaw tightened, and he quickly took the cup from her, so quickly that the delicate china rattled in its saucer. "Thank you, Miss Barclay," he said stiffly, formally.

Her smile disappeared, and she nodded coolly.

Chapter Five

On the sudden,
A Roman thought hath struck him.
　　　　　　　　—*Antony and Cleopatra*

Julia turned away to reach for her own teacup, a bit nonplussed.

Before she met the new Lord Ellston (somehow she could not stop thinking of him as the *new* earl), she had thought he was probably a great prig. A dreadful high stickler. What other kind of person would break with his own father just because that father married an actress? And then to stay away for years!

Julia was not accustomed to priggish people. For that reason, she had not really looked forward to meeting him at all.

But then, he had not seemed so priggish when she met him in the lane. She had caused him to be thrown from his horse, to fall in the mud and become absolutely filthy. Any other man in his situation would have been furious. And she rather suspected he *had* been angry at first.

Then he had laughed. He had even flirted with her. He had treated the whole awful scene as a country lark. It had been almost—fun.

Until she realized who he truly was.

She had tried not to show it to Abelard and the others, but she had been quite nervous at the thought of what could happen when Lord Ellston arrived at Rosemount. He had been kind and flirtatious with a strange girl on the road. How would he behave with Anna Barclay's daughter?

She had always suspected that he would behave as he had four years ago in the library, hurling angry words and accusations. This had been the image she carried with her through those years. Yet he had surprised her again. Once the shock of their introduction waned and they settled down before the fire, he had seemed pensive. Far away from the present moment. Carried off by the enchanted spell Rosemount could sometimes weave, a spell Julia herself knew all too well.

He was obviously startled when she spoke to him, and recalled himself. Recalled the truth of their odd, and rather awkward, situation. His warm blue eyes had turned gray with frost.

He looked a bit like the prig she'd always imagined.

She fought the urge to move closer to the warmth of the fire and instead offered the plate of sandwiches she had been arranging and rearranging. "Would you care for a sandwich, Lord Ellston?" she asked. "I fear supper was over long ago. We keep country hours here. Though, of course, now you must arrange the household schedule to suit your own needs."

She decided not to mention the fact that supper was generally just an extension of the tea, cakes, and sometimes even champagne that were served in the afternoon, after rehearsals. No need to make him think she was a poor household manager just yet.

"Thank you, Miss Barclay," he said, accepting one of the thin-cut cucumber sandwiches. "I prefer country hours myself."

Julia took a rose cream cake. "I suppose you will soon be wanting an accounting of the household."

He smiled at her, still a bit stiff and uncertain, but kindly. "I am sure it is nothing to worry you. I will simply speak to the housekeeper later in the week."

She bit her lip in consternation. "I fear, well, that there is no housekeeper at present. But I can answer any questions you may have." Mrs. Thompson, like her husband, had been rather less than useful. Julia had practically run everything after her mother died.

Marcus paused in lifting his sandwich to his mouth. "No housekeeper at Rosemount?"

"No. You see, Mrs. Thompson had to leave us rather suddenly. But I have all the books and keys, which are, of course, at your disposal."

He frowned, his dark, silky brows almost meeting over his aquiline nose. She feared he might bellow, as Gerald sometimes had when very vexed. He just nodded. "Perhaps tomorrow we could discuss it, then, Miss Barclay. And later in the week maybe you could show me the household books."

"Yes. Certainly." Julia placed her cup carefully back on the table, suddenly very weary. "Now, if you will excuse me, Lord Ellston, I am rather tired."

"Of course. Do forgive me for keeping you so late." Marcus rose with her and walked to the drawing room door.

Elly, Julia's *real* maid, waited there to light her way upstairs.

"If you will ring for Ab-Douglas whenever you are ready," Julia told him, "he will see you to your chamber."

"Yes. Douglas," Marcus answered slowly. "Tell me, Miss Barclay. Exactly how long has Douglas served as butler here?"

"Oh," she said airily, "simply eons. He is a treasure. Good night, Lord Ellston."

"Good night, Miss Barclay."

Julia quickly ascended the staircase, fighting the urge to look back over her shoulder. She could feel his gaze on her until she reached the deep shadows at the top of the stairs.

She was thoroughly exhausted by the time she reached her room. It had been a very long, very odd day, and she just wanted to hide beneath her warm bedclothes and forget all about it.

Sleep, however, was apparently not to be in her near future. Mary and Daphne were waiting for her, playing piquet at the little French card table that had been her mother's, still dressed in their black housemaids' frocks.

"There you are at last!" Mary cried, her blond curls positively atremble with enthusiasm.

"We have been waiting for you for an age," added Daphne. "We want to hear all about it."

Julia dismissed Elly and went to sit at the table with the girls. She kicked off her slippers and stretched her stockinged toes out toward the grate. "All about what?"

Mary giggled. "Your meeting with his lordship, of

course! He is awfully handsome. Just like this Italian opera singer I knew once. Alfredo was his name. . . ."

"What is *really* important," Daphne interrupted, since Mary tended to go on for a long time about her beaux, "is, does he suspect our little ruse?" Unlike her character, the silly shepherdess Phebe, Daphne was quite practical.

Julia shook her head. "I do not think so. Though he did comment on 'Douglas's' oddness as a butler. I think Abby would be quite insulted if he knew he was anything less than thoroughly convincing!"

"Quite so."

"But I think that Lord Ellston rather expected my mother to run an eccentric household and is not surprised. So I'm sure we are safe enough for the present."

"Just as long as we can stay here until next month," Daphne said. "Then we will go on our tour, and all will be well."

"It *would* be nice if we could come back here for Christmas, though," Mary said wistfully. "I haven't had a real country Christmas since I was a girl."

"I doubt even I shall be here for Christmas," Julia answered.

"Why?" asked Daphne. "Where are you going?"

Julia shrugged. "I have no idea as yet. Perhaps with all of you!"

"Oh, that will be such fun!" Mary enthused. "It's always so jolly on tour. So many new admirers . . ."

Daphne looked at Julia slyly. "But rather a pity to leave here when the handsome earl is just arrived, eh, Jule?"

"He is handsome," Julia agreed with a reluctant

laugh. "I think, though, that he wants as little to do with me as possible. Especially after our unfortunate first meeting in the lane!"

"First meeting?"

"Oh, do tell us what happened!"

"No, no," said Julia. "It is far too late, and I am far too tired. And you two will have to be up early to do the dusting!"

Daphne groaned. "How awful! When will we ever have time to rehearse?"

"I'll tell Lord Ellston that the morning room is being redecorated and he shouldn't go in there. That should give you some time in the afternoons, when he is out riding, or whatever it is gentlemen do. Now, good night, dears."

"Good night!" Daphne and Mary chorused. They left the room still whispering and laughing, and shut the door behind them, leaving Julia in quiet at last.

She stood up and went to go look out her window. It was a clear night, with many stars and a nearly full moon bathing the garden in their pale glow.

Julia leaned her forehead against the cool glass. Daphne and Mary were right—Marcus *was* handsome, and when he was near she felt an undeniable sense of odd breathlessness, an almost overwhelming urge to simper and giggle. To run her fingers through his curls and see if they were as soft as they looked.

A more romantical sort might say she was falling in love, or at least in passion, with him.

But Julia was not particularly romantical. That sort of thing was for plays and books, and she could ill afford it in real life. Not at this moment in her life, anyway, when things were so very uncertain. Assuredly not with Marcus Hadley!

"He is not at all the sort of man I admire," she told herself stoutly. Even on their short acquaintance she could tell that he was conventional and more straitlaced than anyone who had traveled so much had a right to be. He was the sort who would go to those staid routs at the Flemings' Belvoir Abbey and *like* them. The sort who would be furious if he discovered she had filled his house with "vulgar" actors.

But, oh, he *was* handsome! And he had such an angelic smile, with a little dimple in his chin. . . .

Julia jerked the draperies closed over the window, shutting off the view of the garden. It was obvious that the moonlight was addling her mind.

Marcus sat in the silence of the drawing room long after Julia left. He stared into the dying fire, sipping absently at his now-cold tea.

The room seemed a great deal more vast, and quieter, without Julia Barclay in it. She was not a loud person, not vulgar and pushing, as he had imagined theater folk might be. But she still seemed to fill the room with her presence, with a certain warmth, and even a sparkle that was gone as soon as she left.

Very peculiar, indeed.

Marcus sighed and sat back wearily in his chair. It was the fatigue causing such fanciful thoughts. Or perhaps that old wag Shakespeare popping up so often in one day, when Marcus hadn't so much as thought about a play or sonnet since Oxford. Yes, it was just the Bard calling up such thoughts of fairies and enchantments, when there was absolutely no room for such things in his life.

Ever since he was a small child, Marcus had a plan for his life. These plans were born and nourished on his mother's tales of how he was the product of two great, ancient families. She exhorted him from the cradle to do fine things to honor that legacy, and so he always had. He excelled in his studies, was enthusiastic at cricket and the hunt, and was well liked by his peers. He had seen his life as following that path forever after—a respectable wife, a nursery full of sons and heirs, perhaps even a career in politics. His mother was proud of him, and, so he assumed, was his father.

And if something elusive was missing in his life, in his heart, well—this was the existence he was born to have, and he could only make the best of it.

So he did. After all, he always did what was expected of him.

Then his mother had died. His approving audience vanished forever, and his father did what was assuredly *not* expected of him.

He married an actress.

Marcus ran his hand through his close-cropped curls, still shaken by the memory of all those emotions that had pummeled him then, even all these years later. His father's actions had seemed a stark betrayal of all Marcus's mother had stood for, all he had thought their entire family stood for.

All that Marcus himself tried so hard to uphold, for them.

The knowledge that his father valued other things above family history and honor had shown Marcus that perhaps he had never known his father at all. Not really.

His whole life, up until then so secure and unshaken, had crumbled into confusion. He had no longer been sure of himself at all. So he, being young and heedless, fled rather than face his troubles.

Marcus reached for the brandy the butler had left on the table and tipped the last of it into his empty teacup. Facing demons was thirsty work.

Well, he had learned a great deal in his wanderings. One of them was that regrets over the past were utterly useless. Yes, he had hoped to make things up to his father. It was too late for him to tell his father how sorry he was, but there was one thing he could do. He could look after the daughter of his father's wife. Not the way he had vaguely thought to look after a child, with governesses and schools. But with a Season, and with finding her a respectable match with a worthy young man.

He felt a rather sour pang at the thought of marching the pretty young woman down the aisle to some respectable baron or younger son. But he quickly shrugged that off.

He would do his duty. Even if her hazel eyes did linger in his mind.

"My lord," the butler said, for once not booming.

Marcus looked up, startled. He had been so wrapped up in his thoughts that he had not even heard the man come into the room. "Yes?"

"Shall I clear away the tray now?"

"What? Oh, yes. I was just preparing to retire."

Marcus watched as the butler stacked the tea things onto a tray and prepared to heft it like a caber. "You said you are a Scot, Douglas?"

Douglas set the tray back down, obviously surprised that Marcus would ask him a question about himself. "Aye, that I am. My lord," he added hastily. "From Aberdeen."

"Were you a butler in Aberdeen?"

Douglas frowned. "I've not been back to Aberdeen in many a year. Not since I was a lad. My lord."

"Miss Barclay tells me that you have been a butler here for a long while."

"Did she, now?" There was a hint of sparkle in Douglas's eyes. "It must be so, then. My lord." Before Marcus could even begin to question him about that odd statement, he continued. "Shall I clear away the table after I see you upstairs, my lord?"

Marcus shook his head. He was far too weary to puzzle out the oddity Rosemount's household had become in his absence. "I assume I will be in my father's old rooms. I remember the way. You can finish in here. I am sorry to keep you so late."

Douglas grinned. " 'Tis no trouble at all, my lord. No trouble at all."

Chapter Six

And then to breakfast with
What appetite you have.

—*Henry VIII*

"Come along, Julia! Just try it. It's quite fun."

"Yes, we just finished polishing it. It is as smooth as satin."

Julia looked down the gleaming length of the banister of the grand staircase. Then she looked up at the eager, exhilarated faces of Mary and Daphne. "I do not know . . ."

"Oh, just try it!"

"You'll like it."

Julia looked at the banister again. She had not slid down it since she had first arrived at Rosemount, four years ago. But she remembered it as being absolutely delightful, like flying. "What if Lord Ellston should see?"

"He won't. He's in the library with some attorney or bailiff, someone terribly official looking."

"We worked so hard at polishing it, Julia!" cried Mary. "It would go to such waste if just Daph and I enjoy it. Well, and Ned; he tried it, too."

Julia laughed. "It will hardly 'go to waste' if I don't slide down it! It is meant to look good, and so it does." But she glanced back over her shoulder at the empty corridor she had just come through on her way to breakfast. Then she peeked down at the foyer; also empty.

She gave in to temptation. Still smiling, she hopped up onto the banister, balancing herself carefully on its smooth surface.

"All right," she said. "Give me a push!"

Daphne gently shoved on her shoulders, and she was off. It *was* like flying, just as she remembered! The air whooshed past her, pulling her hair from its carefully placed pins and sending her skirts fluttering above her ankles.

Daphne and Mary applauded and shouted encouragement. Julia whooped in delight.

Then she landed. Right on top of Lord Ellston, who had chosen just that instant to open the library door and step out into the foyer.

He fell back onto the red-and-blue carpet with a great exhalation of air, Julia sprawled atop him.

Momentarily dazed, she pushed herself up on her elbows and looked down, horrified, into his wide blue eyes.

"My dear Miss Barclay," he gasped. "We must stop meeting this way."

Julia scrambled up off him. "Oh, Lord Ellston! I am so very sorry! Are you injured? Are you—oh, should I send for the doctor?"

"I hardly think that will be necessary." Marcus sat up slowly. "I do believe all my limbs and wits are intact, such as they are."

"I should still send for the doctor," Julia fretted. She glanced up the stairs to see Mary and Daphne staring down at them, pale and startled. She made a small shooing motion with her hand, and they fled into the upstairs corridor. "I might have done you a great injury, Lord Ellston."

With the aid of one of the stout chairs, he managed to pull himself to his feet and stand before her, apparently hale and hearty, if rather disarranged. "I am quite well, I do assure you, Miss Barclay. But under the circumstances, it seems quite ridiculous for us to go on calling each other Lord Ellston and Miss Barclay. Shall we be Marcus and Julia from now on?"

She nodded, and even managed to smile a bit in relief that she had not, for the second time, killed him. "Yes. Of course."

"Well, I am glad we have settled that. I was just on my way to breakfast. Would you join me—Julia?"

"I was just going there, myself—Marcus."

He held out his arm to her politely, as if everything was completely civilized and she had not just flown down the banister to land atop him.

"Thank you," Julia murmured, and slipped her hand into the warm crook of his elbow.

Marcus had awakened early to spend a very long hour with the attorney, going over such dull things as wills, bequests, and entailments. Then he had spent an hour with the bailiff, discussing oats and plowing and tenants. He finally emerged from the library, eagerly in search of his breakfast, only to be knocked flat on his back by a hurtling object.

A hurtling, lavender-scented, blue muslin–clad object.

Somehow, even as he lay breathless on the carpet, he had not been surprised. He had realized the night before that his life had turned tip-over-tail and was not likely to be righted again anytime soon. It seemed all too appropriate that he would start off that new life by being knocked down by a woman sliding down the banister.

As he offered his arm to escort Julia into breakfast, he couldn't help but look back at the staircase gleaming with beeswax in the morning sun. He had only slid down that banister once, when he was seven years old. On that memorable occasion, he had been caught by his nanny and roundly scolded by his mother. Before that scolding, though, he remembered the experience as being rather glorious.

But he had been a little child. Julia Barclay was a grown woman. Supposedly.

He looked down at her as he seated her at the end of the small table in the breakfast room. She looked serene now, her eyes downcast, a polite half smile on her lips. Her hair, though, fell down her back in its profusion of curls, some strands of it still anchored by their pins and combs.

She noticed him noticing, and her cheeks turned bright pink. She reached up and began self-consciously tucking her hair back up.

Marcus smiled and went to take his own seat. He looked about for the breakfast, but the long sideboard was bare of any warming dishes.

Julia, her hair made almost tidy, rang a small bell that sat on her end of the table. "Usually there is a selection laid out for breakfast, Lord—er, Marcus. But I did not know what your preferences are, so I asked the cook to just prepare some eggs, sausage, and toast this morning." She prudently decided not to say that usually breakfast was held late, around ten o'clock, when a pack of ravenous actors fell on the kippers and eggs and ran lines while they ate.

Now they were all hiding in the "being redecorated" morning room, waiting for his lordship to leave so they could rehearse.

All of them except John and Ned. They entered the breakfast room at the sound of the bell, bearing platters of eggs, sausages, and toast before them as if they were carrying the crown jewels. They wore liveries of their own devising—scarlet velvet doublets and hose, complete with tasseled codpieces. Ned even wore a green satin cap with a long red plume affixed to it, which nodded into the eggs with every step he took.

Julia groaned and closed her eyes. She longed to run away, to crawl beneath the table and hide! This scheme of hers had been absolute lunacy. They would surely be found out in no time, and then all of them would be tossed out in the lane clutching their caps and codpieces. Julia included.

But there was no outcry, no shout from Marcus, no crash of crockery. Only the soft sounds of china being laid on the tablecloth, of chocolate and coffee being poured out.

Julia dared to open her eyes and look about cautiously.

John was arranging a fluffy pile of scrambled eggs into artistic little hillocks, while Ned placed a plate of toast and a small crystal jar next to Marcus.

"Excellent. Marmalade. You know, I always missed

this when I was traveling in Egypt. They simply have no concept of good marmalade there," Marcus said. Then he smiled at Julia.

She would almost have preferred him to shout at her. Especially when Ned blew her a kiss behind his lordship's back.

Julia groaned again.

"Julia," Marcus said, as he dolloped a spoonful of marmalade onto his toast, "you must be quite familiar with the grounds and gardens of Rosemount."

Julia frowned, puzzled. The gardens? Whatever did that have to do with marmalade? "Well, yes. I go walking every day."

"Perhaps you would be so good as to walk with me this afternoon? I am sure things must have changed greatly at Rosemount since I have been away. In many ways."

"Of course. Shall we say, after luncheon?"

"Most satisfactory. Oh, and one other thing."

Julia longed to close her eyes again. So here it was. He wanted to know why the housemaids were incompetent, why the footmen looked like they were on their way to Hampton Court to meet Queen Elizabeth, and what the odd noises from the morning room were.

She swallowed. "Yes, Marcus?"

"You may want to speak with the cook. The toast is burned, the coffee is cold, and I could vow that I just bit down on an eggshell."

Julia looked down at her own plate to see that the toast was charred so black that no amount of marmalade could ever hide it.

*   *   *

"What were you doing parading in there as if you were presenting roast peacock to Henry VIII?" Julia leaned back against the closed door of the morning room-cum-theater and eyed Ned and John sternly. "You will have us all found out. I am sure he thought something was most odd."

Ned smiled at her cajolingly. "Ah, Julia. No, he didn't. Not that one. He was too concerned with his burned toast, and with ogling you, to worry about the footmen."

He was ogling her? Julia was intrigued, but she refused to be distracted. "Nevertheless—"

"Besides, Julia," John interrupted, "you told us to use some costumes, since there's no livery for us."

"True," Julia sighed. "I did hope, though, that you could find something more appropriate than the Capulets."

"It was either these or our *As You Like It* forest garb," Ned protested. "Agnes is still mending our things from *Twelfth Night*."

"Those would not have worked, anyway," said John. "It's just more hose and doublets."

Mary and Daphne, who had been silently watching the conversation, nodded in agreement.

"Perhaps you could wear cloaks?" suggested Mary. "Or some powdered wigs."

"Yes!" said Ned. "Footmen do wear powdered wigs, don't they?"

"No! Not with doublets," cried Julia, suddenly weary. "Do not wear cloaks or powdered wigs. That would only call more attention to you. I suppose you must go on wearing your doublets." She looked around the room, at the actors gathered about on the stage and seated on the chairs and settees. Everyone was there, except . . . "Where are Abelard and Charlie?"

"I think Abby was polishing some silver," Daphne said. "He really seems to enjoy that little butler's pantry."

"And Charlie was down in the kitchen, helping prepare luncheon," added Mary.

"I'll speak with them later, then. I need to talk to the cook, anyway, about the dreadful breakfast." Julia climbed onto the stage and sat down on the edge of it, dangling her legs until her feet almost touched the floor. "Tell me, have you had any difficulties with the staff?"

"None at all!" answered Mary. "They all seem to think it great fun, as long as his lordship doesn't find out. Makes a change from dusting and polishing."

"Just as dusting and polishing makes a change from rehearsing!" Daphne said, with a laugh. "This has been a wonderful experience, Julia, for the next time I play the role of a maid. You were so clever to think of such a ruse!"

"I do not feel clever," Julia murmured. "I feel as if we are on the verge of discovery—and disaster."

Mary sat down beside her, suddenly serious. "Why, Julia? Has his lordship implied that he knows what we are about?"

"Not yet," Julia answered. "But I know he knows something odd is afoot. He wants me to take a walk with him after luncheon."

"Perhaps he's going to say he's about to take himself off to London," Ned suggested hopefully. "Then we will all be free to go about as we did before!"

Julia expected to feel only relief at the thought of Marcus leaving. Instead, she felt an odd, rather disappointed pang. "Perhaps. Well, I suppose I will find out after luncheon. Shall we meet again this evening?"

"Yes, after his lordship has gone off to bed!" said John. "Then you can tell us the plans for tomorrow."

"Yes. Tomorrow." Julia leaped down from the stage. "Now I must go speak with the cook about this morning's so-called breakfast. I don't know what could have happened. Her cooking is usually so excellent."

Julia did not even have to summon the cook to her little book room. The buxom Mrs. Gilbert arrived there on her own, her broad face deep crimson with anger, and poor Charlie Englehardt, her temporary "assistant," held firmly by the ear.

"Mrs. Gilbert!" Julia cried, deeply shocked. The household accounts she had been perusing fell back down onto her desk, unheeded. "Whatever is the matter?"

"*This* is the matter, Miss Barclay!"

Mrs. Gilbert shook Charlie firmly, causing him to shout out, "Ow, ow, ow!"

"I have been cook here for over six years," Mrs. Gilbert continued. She finally released Charlie, who fell into a pitifully moaning heap at her feet. "I have prepared supper parties for one hundred guests. I have made lobster patties and mushroom tarts for balls at only a day's notice. I even baked your own mother's wedding cake, miss! And I never thought to be subjected to such indignities in my own kitchen! Not at Rosemount." Tears sprang to her eyes and were wiped hastily away with the hem of her apron. "Do you want my notice, miss?"

"Oh, no!" Julia leaped up in near panic. "No, Mrs. Gilbert, never. Why, you are the finest cook in the county. Everyone says so. Haven't the Hallsbys tried to steal you away numerous times? We would never want to lose you. Please, sit down and tell me what the trouble is. I promise I will do my very best to solve it."

Somewhat mollified, Mrs. Gilbert lowered her girth onto a satin armchair. She treated Charlie, still moaning on the floor, to a disdainful sniff. "I understood when you explained the need for your . . . friends to assist with the household duties for a few days, miss. God knows I am a Christian soul and would never want people to be tossed out to starve. And your mother, God rest her soul, was so good to us, with such high wages and an extra half day off every month, that I can only hope to repay her in some small way."

"That is very good of you, Mrs. Gilbert," Julia said.

"*But*, no one ever said I had to let that . . . that jackanapes into my kitchen!" Mrs. Gilbert's voice swiftly rose again in volume. "I thought he would just sit quietly in the corner, maybe help Betty with peeling some potatoes."

Julia was rather confused. "Is that not what he did?"

"No!" Mrs. Gilbert wailed. "He hid in the cupboard and scared poor Betty so that she burned the toast. Then, while she was in hysterics, he sent the toast out with those footmen of yours. I set him to whisking eggs, and he mixed in eggshells with them. He took the coffee off the stove where it was to warm and let it go cold. Because of *him*, his lordship thinks I can't make a simple thing like breakfast! I'll get the sack for certain, and it'll be me starving in the road."

Julia listened to this litany of complaints in stunned silence. "Oh, no, Mrs. Gilbert! I am sure there is no question of anyone getting the, er, sack. I told Lord Ellston that you are a superb cook and that something must have gone terribly wrong in the kitchen this morning. I am certain that he will see what I meant when he eats the wonderful luncheon you are no doubt preparing."

"Well," huffed Mrs. Gilbert, obviously beginning to be mollified, "I *am* making my salmon croquettes, and then a nice beef boulogne for supper. And maybe an apricot tart for dessert."

"Excellent!" Julia said enthusiastically. "I know Lord Ellston will be most appreciative."

Mrs. Gilbert deigned to give a small smile. "I will not be able to do my best salmon croquettes, though, if *that* is allowed in my kitchen." She pointed at Charlie, who rolled onto his back as if mortally wounded.

Julie eyed him dispassionately. "Yes, I do see what

you mean, Mrs. Gilbert. Have no fear. I will send Charlie to work in the stables."

"The stables!" Charlie shouted, only to fall back down at Julia's stern look.

"So you may tell Betty that she can go on with her work unmolested," Julia continued. "If that will be satisfactory, Mrs. Gilbert?"

"Quite satisfactory, Miss Barclay." Mrs. Gilbert rose and straightened her apron, her feathers now smoothed. "I will just be getting on with luncheon, then."

As soon as the door shut behind her, Charlie sat straight up. " 'Thou marble-hearted fiend!' " he shouted at the door.

Julia frowned at him. "I don't want to hear another word out of you, Charlie Englehardt. Especially not *King Lear*. You behaved very badly."

Charlie crawled toward her on his knees, his hands clasped beseechingly. "Oh, Julia, sweet Julia! I beg you, don't send me to the stable! My delicate hands were never made for mucking out stalls."

"You should have thought of that before you were such a nodcock in the kitchen. What would we have done if Mrs. Gilbert had indeed resigned? None of us can cook."

"I was only trying to brighten her day with a bit of humor. How was I to know the kitchen maid would burn the toast? It won't happen again, Julia, I vow!"

Julia shook her head sternly. "We can't afford to have any of the real staff quit. So to the stables with you, Charlie. For today, at least. You can polish tack or some such. Just *don't* bother the horses."

"But . . ."

"Not another word! To the stables."

After Charlie departed, grumbling, Julia buried her face in her hands and groaned. So many crises averted already, and it wasn't even noon yet.

What could the rest of the day possibly hold?

Chapter Seven

Here's flowers for you;
Hot lavender, mints, savoury marjoram;
The marigold, that goes to bed wi' the sun,
And with him rises weeping.

—*The Winter's Tale*

"Tell me, Julia, do you like living at Rosemount?"

Julia, who had turned away to examine one of the flower beds in the garden, looked back at Marcus in surprise. He had been so very quiet during their walk, up until now. "Do I—what?"

"Like living at Rosemount. Are you happy here?"

"Of course I am," she answered slowly, bemused by both the question and the way the sun turned his black hair to the sheen of a raven's wing. She blinked quickly. "Who could fail to be happy at Rosemount?"

"Who, indeed? May I ask where you lived before you came here?"

"Oh, noplace really."

"Noplace?" he said, startled.

"I do not mean we lived in a gypsy wagon or anything of that sort," Julia clarified. "We had a house in London. Mother often had engagements there during the Season. But usually she was on tour. I saw all of England and a great deal of Wales, Ireland, and Scotland before I was twelve years old. It was very exciting, to be sure, and I would not trade those experiences for anything. It is just . . ." Her voice trailed away, and she looked out over the neat gardens wistfully.

How she loved every rosebush, every statue, every lavender border! She hated the thought of leaving it all, of being rootless again.

"It is just that such a wandering life is not the same as having a *real* home, is it?" Marcus said quietly.

Julia's gaze flew up to his. His expression was solemn as he looked at her, and very, very understanding.

Ever since their meeting in the drawing room yesterday, Julia had felt nervous around him. After all, he held the power to send her away from her home. She had not wanted to trust his flashes of humor, his charming smiles.

But *this* Marcus, so serious and understanding, she somehow felt she could trust. This Marcus gazed at Rosemount with all the longing she herself felt. He had seen so much, just as she had, and knew the wonderful thing this place was.

Did he also know the value of peace?

Deeply confused, Julia sat down on a nearby bench set in the shade of a tall tree. She put her basket of flowers down at her feet and carefully folded her hands on her lap.

"Nothing is the same as having a real home," she said. "As having a place to belong to, to be safe in. I did not really mind the travel, you see, because I was with my mother. She was my family, my home. When I lost her, it was a great comfort to be here at Rosemount, where we had been so happy."

Marcus nodded. "I felt the same when I lost my

own mother. I felt that a part of her remained here. I feel that still."

"Yes!" Julia cried. "Yes, that is it exactly."

"I am glad that you have found comfort here, Julia."

"And I hope that you may do so, Marcus. Now that you are home again."

"Thank you."

They looked at each other then, and Julia fancied she saw a tenderness in his face that had not been there before. An openness. Emboldened, she leaned toward him and said, "Please, Marcus, I must ask you something."

"What is it?"

"I know that one day you . . . you will marry, and that perhaps that day will be soon. I only want to ask, to beg, that you not send me away right away. That you give me time to make arrangements that I would find agreeable."

His eyes widened in surprise. "Send you away?"

"If my being here at the house is in some way uncomfortable for you, I could remove to the dower house," she rushed on. She had only thought of the dower house last night. It was rather small for herself and all the actors, but they could manage. She would still be at Rosemount, could still walk in the gardens.

But she could see that he was appalled by the idea. Perhaps he had some old auntie he wanted to move into the dower house.

"If that does not suit, there is also a cottage to let in the village," she said. "Though I fear I have no money until I receive the bequest your father promised me for a dowry. If—"

"Julia!" Marcus interrupted. "Julia, please. I know that you have little reason to trust in me. But please know that I would never turn you out to a cottage or the dower house."

Julia's burgeoning hysterics stilled. "You would not?"

"I am not some ogre. In the spring I intend to take you to my cousin, Lady Thornton, in London. She will sponsor you for the Season. My father did leave you a substantial dowry, and I will see to all the additional expenses of clothing and a come-out ball. So you need not worry about anything."

Then Marcus sat back with a smile, obviously expecting her to shower him with gratitude.

Julia feared that her mouth was inelegantly agape as she stared at him.

A *Season*? The great lout thought to placate her with a Season? And here she had foolishly thought they were understanding each other so well. That he knew how deeply she dreaded leaving Rosemount. Yet here he smugly sat, thinking a jaunt to London, a chance to snare a husband, would make everything right with her.

Julia did not trust herself to speak just at that moment. She looked back out at the garden, but now she took little pleasure in the autumn flowers there.

Her mother and Gerald had talked about a London Season, of course. They had wanted to open up Hadley House on Grosvenor Square again, to throw lavish balls and routs in her honor. After all, as her mother pointed out, she would have to marry one day, and there was a distinct paucity of eligible gentlemen in the neighborhood.

Julia, however, had known that she would never find the sort of man she would like among Town bucks and beaux. She had finally compromised by agreeing to go with them to Bath next summer instead, and look about there.

Since her mother's passing, she had given up the thought of any kind of Season, and not without a measure of relief. She was perfectly content to be at home with her books and her own kind of friends.

Now here was Marcus, declaring that all her troubles were at an end because he, her shining knight, was going to send her off to London!

She would much rather go live in the cottage.

However, she could not just smack him over the head with her basket as she longed to do. She had to tread carefully. And, she told herself, spring was months away. Anything could happen between now and then.

She pasted on a bright smile and turned back to him. "A Season. Well. How good of you to think of me. But I pray that you will not go to any difficulties on my behalf."

His own confident smile faltered. "It is no difficulty at all, I assure you."

Julia shook her head. "I would never want to be a burden to you. A Season is so much trouble, such expense! I am really too old, you know, and I am sure I would not take. But it is so good of you to think of it!" She gathered up her basket and stood. "It is becoming rather warm out, and I have letters to write before supper. If you will excuse me?"

Marcus bowed. "Certainly. We can speak further about this at supper."

"Yes, of course. At supper." She nodded and smiled again, then hurried off toward the safety of the house. If she had *her* wish, they would never speak of it again.

Marcus watched Julia's blue-clad figure as she marched down the pathway, her back as stiff and straight as a soldier's. Every twitch of her skirt, every jerk of her head, spoke of her irritation.

Women! If he lived to be a hundred, he would never understand them.

He sat back down on the bench and ran his hands through his hair leaving the short curls sticking straight. He was too confused by the enigma that was Julia Barclay.

Why would she be angered by his offer of a Season? Any other woman would have been overjoyed at the chance to go to Town, to attend parties and have someone else pay the bills. Any other woman would have been relieved to know that someone was looking out for her welfare, for her future.

Not Julia. He had the distinct impression that she was disappointed by his plans. Her hazel eyes had flashed furiously at him before she quickly veiled them in blandness.

Obviously, he had missed something vital, and now she considered him a clumsy cabbage head who had no clue as to what might make a lady truly happy.

That stung a bit. Certainly the ladies he had known in Paris and Florence and Cairo had been happy to receive his thoughtfully considered gifts, and had thanked him very prettily. They had never palmed him off with patently false excuses and then stalked away, as Julia had.

For some reason, he found himself very much wanting to make Julia happy. He wanted her to smile at him again, in the easy way she had when they first met in the lane, before she knew who he was. He wanted her eyes to sparkle with laughter.

And the damnable thing was, his desire to see her happy had nothing to do with any obligation he felt toward his father's memory. Not that he was quite prepared to admit that, even to himself.

How could he possibly find out what would make this woman, who was unlike anyone he had ever known, smile at him again?

"*Then* he offered me a Season!" Julia, who had gone straight from the garden to Agnes's room, cried out the last of her tale. "Can you imagine?"

Agnes smiled gently. "How dare he offer to pay for a Season, to help you find a suitable husband? The cad."

Julia peeked up from where she had buried her face in the cushions of the chaise. "Are you laughing at me?"

"Just a bit, dear. Lord Ellston sounds quite generous to me. Doesn't every girl dream of London balls, of capturing the attention of some handsome beau?"

"Not *this* girl." Julia sat up against the cushions she had been buried in. "I had thought we were coming to understand each other. That he understood why I did not want to leave the neighborhood. I was beginning to think he would even let me move into the dower house. Then he said he was going to send me off to his cousin for the Season, to marry me off! And he looked so smug and satisfied, as if he were some rajah bestowing favors, and I should fall down at his feet in gratitude.''

Agnes laughed. ''Oh, Julia! He *is* a man, you know. You cannot expect a man to understand such subtleties. No doubt the women he has known before *have* fallen at his feet in gratitude for his gifts. I'm sure you are the first one who hasn't, and he doesn't know what to do with you.''

Julia grinned. ''I have no doubt you are right, Agnes. You should have seen him when I refused his offer of a Season! He looked quite like a trout who has suddenly landed out of water. At least we needn't worry about him for very much longer.''

''How so?''

''He told me that Gerald's bequest to me was very generous. When you all leave on tour, I will come with you and look all about England for the most agreeable cottage to purchase. A cottage would be a much better investment than a dowry, I think. Then I shall have a home of my own, just as I have always wanted.'' She plucked at the fringed trim of the cushion as she thought of living in her snug cottage far away from Rosemount. All alone.

''You don't seem terribly enthusiastic about the whole idea,'' Agnes observed.

Julia looked up in surprise. ''Do I not?''

''No. You seem rather . . . wistful. What did you think would happen when Lord Ellston came back to Rosemount?''

Julia shrugged. ''Exactly this, I suppose. That my

life would have to change its course. I just never expected . . ."

"To like Lord Ellston?"

So the truth came out. Yes, she *did* like Marcus. More than she would ever have expected to, more than she wanted to. He had behaved so badly four years ago that she had thought she would despise him. But he was not the arrogant, humorless lout she had imagined.

It made an already complicated situation even worse. She already didn't want to leave Rosemount; it would be terrible if she didn't want to leave Marcus, as well.

"You are too perceptive for my own good, Agnes," she said.

"Just be careful, Julia."

"I am always careful. Especially now that you are all relying on me so."

"It is not that. It is just that, well, that we would hate to see you hurt."

"I will not be hurt. But it is so very nice to have friends to worry about me. I should go change for supper. It is getting late." She blew Agnes an airy kiss and went off down the corridor to her own room.

Elly, her maid, had already been there to build up the fire and lay out a pale yellow silk gown for Julia to wear to supper.

And, on her dressing table, sat a very large bouquet.

It glowed with the autumn colors of the flowers in the gardens, gold and saffron and burgundy. It was tied up with red-and-gold striped ribbons, and a carefully folded note was tucked among the petals.

It was the first bouquet she had ever received from anyone except her stepfather.

She unfolded the note, and read the words scrawled there in a bold, black hand:

My dear Miss Barclay,

Please forgive my presumptuousness of this afternoon. London is indeed not for everyone, as I well know. Perhaps we could discuss any ideas you may have after supper?

Sincerely,
Your friend,
Marcus.

Julia smiled softly, and tucked the note carefully away in her jewel case, to be taken out and reread later.

Chapter Eight

It were all one
That I should love a bright, particular star
And think to wed it, he is so above me.
            —*All's Well That Ends Well*

After an excellent supper, where Mrs. Gilbert's superb beef boulogne and apricot tart proved that peace once again reigned in the kitchen, Marcus and Julia retired to the library for sherry and tea.

It was quiet and cozy in the dark-paneled room, with the green velvet draperies drawn across the windows and a fire blazing in the hearth. It should have all been conducive to easy conversation and amiability, yet their words had been rather strained at supper, and now they sat in silence in each other's company. The memory of the afternoon's misunderstanding still hung heavy between them.

Julia sipped at her sherry and looked about the library. When Gerald was alive it had been his own sanctum, and she had only been in there once in a while, to find new books to read. After he died, she found entering it too painful. It was so full of memories of her stepfather, redolent of the scent of his pipe and echoing with his deep laughter.

Tonight, though, she did not feel the pang of loss. It had become too much Marcus's room, and no longer Gerald's. The smell of pipe tobacco was replaced by the faint citrus tang of Marcus's cologne. His crates had been delivered that afternoon and were stacked along the walls now, spilling out all sorts of exotic, enticing items.

Including the one that now sat on the desk.

Julia was so drawn to it that she forgot Marcus was sitting there watching her. She put her glass down on the table and walked over to examine the object closer.

It was an alabaster sculpture of a woman's head, barely ten inches high but utterly exquisite. Julia ran a careful fingertip over the woman's perfect features. The cold stone of the eyes seemed almost alive, wry and sparkling as the ancient woman looked out on the modern world.

Marcus came up beside Julia quietly, so quietly that she did not even notice him until he spoke, his warm breath gently stirring the curls at her temple.

"Isn't she beautiful?" he said softly.

Julia smiled at him. "Lovely. Where did you get her?"

"In Egypt. I found her in a small shop in Cairo. The proprietor was aghast that I would not bargain with him over the price. I would have paid anything to have this statue."

"I do not blame you." Julia perched herself on the edge of the desk. "It must have been very exciting in Egypt."

Marcus laughed. "I am not sure *exciting* is the word for it. Terrifying at times; dull as tombs at others. It was hot, and travel was very slow. But it was fascinating." He sat down on the chair behind the

desk and leaned his elbow next to Julia, his gaze very
far away. "The food was unlike anything I had ever
eaten. Not like bland English food at all. They used
spices never even heard of here. And the people were
endlessly intriguing."

"Did you see the pyramids? And the temple at
Karnak?"

He smiled up at her. "How do you know about
Karnak, Julia?"

"I am not an uneducated ignoramus, you know. I
have a book about Egypt, with engraved illustrations.
I've spent so many hours looking at them, imagining
what it must be like to actually be there." She did
not tell him that she had bought the book after he
wrote to Gerald from Egypt and Gerald had read the
letter aloud to her. She didn't want to spoil this moment with reminders of what was past. "I should
like to go to Egypt one day. And Italy and France,
maybe even India."

"I think you would like Egypt very much. But did
you not tell me that you only want to be a country
homebody from now on?" he gently teased.

"I *do* want a home," she answered with a laugh.
"A place I can come back to that will always be mine.
That does not mean I want to lock myself into that
home and never leave! I fear I could never entirely
leave behind my wandering youth. Perhaps one day
I *will* go to Egypt!"

"Well, until then . . ." Marcus went to one of the
open crates and rummaged about until he found a
small, wrapped object. He came to her and pressed
it into her hand. "Keep this with you. It will bring
you good fortune."

Julia unwrapped it eagerly. It was a small turquoise beetle, covered with tiny, odd carvings. She turned it over on her palm, to see more of the carvings on its flat belly. "It is a very lovely . . . bug, Marcus."

"It is a scarab," he said. "Carved with magical incantations. You can put it on a chain and wear it, see this tiny hole here? The man I bought it from swore that it would bring good fortune to whoever possesses it."

"Then I must wear it. I could use some good fortune." Julia closed her fist around the scarab and held it very tightly. "Thank you, Marcus."

She looked up to find him watching her intently, his blue eyes almost black in the firelit shadows.

"Julia," he said quietly, "I am very sorry about this afternoon. I was so presumptuous, assuming that you would want to go to London. I should never have made such plans without consulting you."

Julia shook her head. "No, Marcus, *I* am sorry. I behaved like such a spoiled little chit! You were only trying to help me, in the best way that you knew how."

He smiled wryly. "It seems we are fated to be always stumbling and apologizing with each other."

"Oh, no!" she said brightly. "As long as you ask before you pack me off to London, we should never have to apologize again!"

Marcus laughed. "Agreed."

"The flowers were lovely, too, Marcus."

He shrugged. "They were only flowers I picked from the gardens, much to the head gardener's chagrin. They were all I could find at such short notice.

I doubt that there are any respectable florists in Little Dipping!"

"They were more beautiful than any hothouse orchid. I would never complain. At any rate, it was the first bouquet I have ever received except from your father."

"The first bouquet! No, I do not believe you. I am certain the local beaux must shower you with blossoms."

"What local beaux? Eligible *partis* are rather thin on the ground in the neighborhood. Though I do think Mr. Elliott, the new curate, rather likes me."

Marcus frowned. "Well, then, all the more reason why you should go to Town, if the local swains are so blind . . ."

"Ah!" Julia laid her finger lightly against his lips. "Now, you agreed not to mention London."

He smiled. His lips were soft against her finger, the movement of his smile intoxicating. She watched in fascination as the dimple appeared in his chin. She longed to trace her fingers across that dimple, along the sharp line of his jaw, into the softness of his hair. . . .

She pulled back as if burned. What could she have been thinking to touch him like that? Most improper.

He looked as dazed as she felt, his eyes wide and unfocused as he stared at her. "Julia, I . . ." he began, only to have his voice trail away into silence.

Julia understood entirely. What could there be to say?

"I should say good night now," she whispered. "It is late."

"Yes," he said. "I suppose—good night."

Julia nodded. Then she slid down off the desk and tried to walk in a slow, dignified manner out of the library. Once the door shut behind her, she raced up the stairs, fleeing to the safety of her bedchamber.

Julia lay awake late into the night, long after the rest of the household slumbered. She held the scarab tightly in her hand, clutching at the reality of the cool stone because she very much feared that reality was slipping away from her.

Those few moments in the library with Marcus had seemed magical. Like a time out of time. For one brief instant, they had not been the Earl of Ellston and Anna Barclay's daughter; they had just been a man and a woman enjoying each other's company. Attracted to each other.

Or at least *she* had been attracted to *him*. She had felt like she could fall into the sea blue of his eyes and happily drown there.

Then cold reality had intruded, as it always did. They were not just a man and a woman who could meet and talk and flirt and perhaps hope for an understanding. He was the same man who had left home rather than accept her mother into it. She was still the daughter of that actress.

Marcus was not a bad man; she knew that. He was remorseful now for his behavior toward his father. He wanted to do right by her, even if he was not certain what that right could be. She had even been tempted to confide in him that evening, when they had seemed so close in the firelight, to tell him about Abelard and the others, to ask for his help.

Fortunately, she had not been so foolish. Marcus was kind now, but she could not know how far that kindness would reach. He was still an earl, with certain lofty standards to uphold—at least in his own mind. One day he would bring a wife to Rosemount, probably someone like Lady Angela Fleming. He would have little patience with Julia then.

Julia sighed and rolled over onto her side, still clutching the scarab. It was a full moon tonight; the great silvery wash of it fell from her uncurtained window, across the floor. That was probably what was causing these restless thoughts tonight.

For one second, looking at Marcus across his Egyptian statue, she had had the giddy sense that everything was changing between them. In reality, *nothing* had changed at all, except that suddenly her life was far more complicated.

She seemed to be falling in love with Marcus.

"No!" she muttered aloud. "It is not love. It is only moon madness. No one falls in love in two days."

And only the greatest of fools would choose this moment, and this man, to fall in love with. Julia had never considered herself a fool.

She just needed to sleep. After a good night's sleep, everything would be clear again. The light of day would clear away these moon dreams.

The only solution would be to stay away from Marcus as much as possible, to stop these wild feelings before they became painful or dangerous.

She turned her face into the pillow and closed her eyes tightly.

"Ping!"

A sharp, tinny sound echoed across the room. Julia

lifted her head and looked around. There was nothing in the room; not even a mouse scurried across the floor.

So now she was hearing things, as well. Julia laid her head back down with a sigh.

"Ping!"

She did *not* imagine that! Julia threw back the bedclothes and climbed out of bed, reaching for her dressing gown. It sounded like someone was trying to break her window by flinging little pebbles at it.

She opened the casement and peered outside. If this was Mary or Daphne come to draw her into some mischief again . . .

It was not Mary or Daphne, or John or Ned, or any of the actors. It was Marcus, standing below her window bathed in the glow of moonlight. His arm was held back, ready to toss another pebble. At the sight of her, he dropped his arm and smiled up at her sheepishly.

Her heart gave an unwilling little leap at the sight of him there.

"Hello, Julia," he said. "I hope I did not wake you."

"What are you doing?" she whispered loudly. "Do you want to wake the whole house?" Then she frowned suspiciously. "Are you foxed?"

"Of course I am not foxed," he answered indignantly. "I just wanted to talk to you."

"Talk? About what?"

Truth to tell, Marcus was not at all sure what it had been he wanted to talk to her about. It had just seemed urgent that he *did* talk to her.

Well, it had seemed urgent when he was sitting alone in the library, anyway.

He did not like the way they had left things. It had seemed like a new understanding was growing between them. When he looked into Julia's eyes, he had felt he could tell her anything, confide anything in her, and she would understand.

It was a warm, comfortable feeling, even when mixed with the less comfortable sensations of his desire for her, of his nearly overwhelming need to kiss her.

Then the wariness had crept back into her eyes, and she had withdrawn from him.

He understood, of course. Their situation was so odd, so strained. She was right to be uncertain; God knew he was.

But it had pained him, nonetheless. He had wanted to talk to her some more, to restore that comfortable, exciting feeling between them. His life had been so devoid of comfort; he found it to be quite addictive.

Julia was quite addictive.

Marcus rubbed a rueful hand along his jaw. Perhaps he *was* a bit foxed, though he had not really had that much brandy to drink. It would explain why he was behaving in such a wildly uncharacteristic way.

He had never before even vaguely considered going to a woman's window and throwing pebbles at it.

Yet there he was, looking up at Julia in the moonlight.

She looked so lovely, so otherworldly. Her hair fell loose over her shoulders in its cascade of curls. Her white nightdress glistened almost silver. She could have been in truth the angel he had first imagined her.

Except that angels didn't frown.

"I only wanted to say that I am sorry I made you run away from the library so suddenly," he called to her. "I do always seem to be saying the wrong things to you."

Her frown eased. "You did not say the wrong thing, Marcus, or make me run away. It was simply growing late; it was time for me to retire."

"Then you are not angry with me?"

She shook her head. "How could I be angry with you, when you gave me such a lovely gift as the scarab?"

He smiled in relief. "Good. Excellent."

"So, is that all you wanted? To say you're sorry?"

No, that was *not* all he wanted. He wanted so much more from her; to kiss her, and touch the wild fall of her hair, to hold her close. But he could never tell her that. It seemed that all his new tangle of emotions from this strange night would have to stay locked up inside him.

"Yes," he answered. "That was all I wanted."

"Well, you could have told me that in the morning," she said, her voice full of laughter.

"Did I wake you, Julia?"

"No," she admitted. "I am not really very tired."

"Neither am I."

She perched on the edge of the window ledge, balancing there as she looked down at him. "Would you like to see something special, then?"

He would, indeed. If that something was her. "What is it?"

"Wait there. I'll be down in a moment." She withdrew from the window, and then shut the casement and drew the curtains closed.

Marcus was left alone in the suddenly very silent night.

He sat down on a nearby bench to wait for her, feeling bemused and utterly unlike himself.

What was he doing?

Chapter Nine

The moon shines bright: in such a night as this,
When the sweet wind did gently kiss the trees
And they did make no noise.
                              —*The Merchant of Venice*

"What are you *doing*, girl?" Julia muttered to herself, as she pulled a simple muslin morning dress over her head and looked around for her half boots. "You just vowed to be sensible, and now you are running off into the night with *him*?"

She *had* just made up her mind to distance herself from Marcus, to cut off any budding tender feelings before they caused any real trouble. She had resolved to be her own sensible, practical self.

And now what was she doing, not fifteen minutes later? Preparing to go off with him, to show him her own special, secret place.

She was moon mad, indeed.

Well, if she was, then so be it. For just this one night, she would be mad and not fear the consequences. One day, when she was old and alone, she could remember this night, and remember a man with eyes as blue as the sea who shared it with her.

"'Let us be Diana's foresters, gentlemen of the shade, minions of the moon,'" she murmured as she swirled her red woolen cloak over her shoulders.

*   *   *

"Where are we going?" Marcus asked as Julia led him across the meadows and along a narrow lane.

"I told you, it is a surprise," she said. "You will see it when we get there. It is a special place."

"A special place, eh? I walked this lane many times as a boy; I would vow I know every special place for miles around."

Julia laughed and shook her head. "I would vow you do not know this one! It is very well hidden." She ducked off of the lane suddenly and into the woods, her red cloak fading into the shadows. "Hurry up, now!" she called. "You would not want to get lost."

She reached for his hand then, and led him deeper into the woods, following a seemingly directionless path.

Marcus almost asked her again where they were going but then thought better of it. The moment was too perfect to ruin with words. Julia's fingers were warm and soft as they grasped his; her lavender scent was sweet. Her hair fell over her shoulders in a loose cloud of curls, and in the moonlight she looked in truth like a fairy being. An unearthly sprite who would vanish with the dawn, instead of the angel he had fancied her earlier.

She tugged him through a break in the trees, and he saw their destination at last.

It was an ancient circle of stones, laid out carefully in a small clearing. The standing stones glowed in the darkness with an almost palpable magic.

Marcus shook his head. Lud, but when had he become so fanciful? Angels, fairies, now magic stones. There must have been some odd mushrooms in that mushroom-and-spinach tart at supper, that were affecting his senses.

But he knew, in his heart, that it was not some mushroom, or the brandy he had drunk, that was causing such romantical thoughts. It was Julia.

She stood close to him, her head just barely reaching to his shoulder. One long, soft curl touched his arm as she whispered, "Is it not beautiful?"

"Yes," he whispered back, watching her face. "Beautiful."

Marcus was as affected by the stones as she was, Julia could tell. He stared at the ring solemnly, his eyes glistening.

"Isn't it glorious?" she said quietly.

"I have never seen anything like it," he answered. "Not in all the places I have been. I didn't even know it was here."

"Soon after I arrived at Rosemount, one of the old local farmers told me about it. He said that legend has it that it was built by the fairy folk, and as I had the eyes of one of 'the wee ones,' I should see it. Of course, I was enchanted by it." She looked around at the familiar, sheltering stones. "It became my own special, secret place, where I could come whenever I was sad or afraid or even very, very happy. I have never shown it to anyone before."

He looked at her in surprise. "Not to anyone?"

"No."

"Then I am very honored indeed that you have brought me here."

"Well, you have the eyes of the wee ones, as well."

Julia smiled at him and walked into the circle of stones. She touched the tallest one, laying her palm flat against the cool surface. "It must seem rather paltry to you, after the pyramids of Egypt. It is not even as large as Stonehenge!"

"Perhaps not, but I think your farmer was right—it must have been built with the magic of the fairy folk." Marcus sat down on one of the flat stones and looked around him in wonder. It *was* enchanted, and unlike anything he had ever seen before.

Just as Julia was unlike any other person he had ever known. She didn't smile coyly, like other women he had known, or flirt and laugh in any practiced way. She was only herself. Like now, as she twirled about in the moonlight, her red cloak swirling like that of an ancient priestess invoking the moon goddess.

"When I was a child," she said, "my mother read me plays instead of storybooks. Shakespeare, mostly, whatever she was rehearsing. And *A Midsummer Night's Dream* was my very favorite then. I would tell my mother that one day I was going to run away to live with the fairies. I made her call me Peaseblossom for a while." She sat down beside him, her cloak settling around her in a soft woolen puddle. "I could envision Titania and Oberon living here. I could almost feel myself back in my childhood. With my mother."

She looked away, but not before he saw the unshed tears shimmering in her eyes.

A pang of guilt touched Marcus's heart. "You must miss her very much."

"Yes. I also miss Gerald. Just as you do. He was so kind to me."

He *did* miss his father. But what he missed the most was not what they had had, which had always been rather distant, but what they might have had if he had stayed at Rosemount, as he should have, and accepted his father's new wife. Perhaps then they could have been truly close, as Marcus had always wished for them to be.

"Yes," he said. "Julia, I know that you have little reason to trust me, as I said before. I behaved so badly in the past. But I hope you know that I would like to be your friend, if you will let me."

She looked up at him, her lips parted in a little "o" of surprise. "We are friends, Marcus. Or why else would I have brought you here?" She touched his arm, oh so lightly, like a butterfly landing, but it felt as if all the warmth of the sun lay there. "Somehow I felt like you needed its magic as much as I do."

Marcus had the overwhelming urge to pull her into his arms, to bury his face in her soft hair and lose all worries and responsibilities in her warmth. He wanted to stay like this, sitting beside her on these magic stones, in the moonlight, forever.

Instead, he looked away from her, rubbing his hand over his eyes. He should not be thinking this way. No matter how pretty, how unique Julia Barclay was, or how enchanted he was by her company, he could not afford these feelings.

She was not at all the sort of woman to make a suitable Countess of Ellston—sophisticated, pedigreed, a grand Society hostess. Julia was none of those things, but oh, how she made him laugh! Made him feel alive, truly alive, in ways he never had. But he had a duty and a name to uphold, a duty he had been taught all his life. He couldn't just abandon it, as his father had.

Could he?

Julia was staring up at him, her forehead wrinkled in concern.

"We should be getting back to the house," he said. "You will catch a chill here in the night air."

"It is not cold," she answered quietly. "I have my cloak."

"Nevertheless, I would never forgive myself if you became ill."

She nodded and slid down off the rock, turning her steps back to the narrow pathway. "Perhaps it is cold, after all," she said. Then she looked back at him over her shoulder, straight into his eyes as if she could see right into his very soul. "But I want you to know, Marcus, that you can come back here whenever you like. Its magic is always present."

She walked quickly away, forcing him to rush after her or be left behind.

Julia hurried along the lane, trying not to listen to the crunch of Marcus's footsteps behind her, or feel the warmth of him at her back.

He had been so kind, so understanding earlier; why was he suddenly so distant? Why did she feel like whenever she came close to a glimpse of Marcus, the *real* Marcus, the Marcus she could admire, he skittered away from her? Hid behind the cool blue of his eyes.

He would seem to want so much to confide in her, to be close to her. Then he would retreat into formality.

Why? Why would he do that, when she so wanted to be his friend? To help him heal some of the pain she sensed he held in his heart.

But she feared she knew the answer to that already. It was because she was the daughter of Anna Barclay, the actress. She was not a "proper" lady, and all of his upbringing held him back, reminded him of his duty. Somehow he could not break free, as Gerald had.

And Julia did not know how to help him. She could only hope that the stones would work their ancient magic and bring him some relief.

At first she did not hear the sound of the vehicle coming along the lane behind them, so deep in her thoughts was she. Then the noise of the horses and the wheels penetrated her melancholy fog, and she realized how scandalous it would look, her and the Earl of Ellston alone on a country lane after midnight.

She grabbed Marcus's arm and pulled him with her into the shadows of the trees that lined the lane.

"Who is it?" Marcus whispered.

"I do not know," she whispered back, straining to see who it was coming up the lane. All she could tell was that it was a small, black, open landau. "No matter who it is, though, you would not want to be seen here with me, alone, would you?"

"I quite see your point."

His warm breath stirred one of her loose curls against her nose, causing a sneeze to well up. It escaped in a great "Choo!" just as the landau came up alongside their hiding place.

"Did you hear something, Mr. Elliott?" asked the vicar, Mr. Whitig, to his curate.

Mr. Andrew Elliott turned his handsome blond head, and Julia feared for a moment that he could see them there.

But he just said, "It was probably an owl, Mr. Whitig."

"No doubt. I do hate these late-night errands. I fear I am becoming too old for the chill night air."

Then they were gone, the landau rolling off down the road.

Julia sighed in relief. "Thank the stars they didn't see us!"

"The vicar?"

"Mr. Whitig is the biggest gossip in the neighborhood," she said, starting to walk again toward home. "He just can't seem to help himself. And, unfortunately for any malefactors, he is in the best position to know all the *on dits,* and spread them far and wide. After all, he does marry, christen, and bury everyone."

Marcus fell into step beside her. "Who was that man with him?"

"The handsome blond one? That was Mr. Elliott, the curate. He hasn't been with us very long. He is quite the local beau ideal."

Marcus felt an unpleasant frisson of jealousy. Julia found the curate handsome? "Is he your beau ideal, too, Julia?"

She just laughed and quickened her steps through Rosemount's garden.

"Faith, and will you look at that?" Abelard said as he looked out the morning room window. He had gone to close the draperies but was arrested by the sight he saw.

Julia and his lordship were walking along the garden path, talking with their heads bent together.

"What is it?"

Mary and John, who had been rehearsing a scene, abandoned their scripts to come and peer over his shoulder.

"Well," Mary breathed. "Julia and his lordship out strolling in the moonlight."

"Who would have thought that stuck-up lordship had it in him?" said John.

As they watched, Marcus lifted Julia's hand to his lips for a brief salute before they parted and went their separate ways.

For just one instant, Marcus's face was illuminated by the moonlight as he watched Julia leave. His expression was very telling indeed, a spasm of tenderness and longing. Then a cool, expressionless mask descended on his features, and he turned away.

Mary, John, and Abelard ducked down until he was safely out of sight.

"Well, Mary and Johnny," Abelard said, rubbing thoughtfully at his ginger whiskers. "Are you thinking the same thing I am thinking?"

"Oh, yes, Abby," Mary answered. "I am sure we are."

John looked at them, puzzled. "What are you thinking?"

Mary just smiled and patted his arm. "Don't you worry about a thing, John. You just do as you're told, and leave the thinking to us. We are going to see everything right for Julia. Are we not, Abby?"

"Indeed we are, Mary dear. Indeed we are."

Chapter Ten

By the pricking of my thumbs,
Something wicked this way comes.
                              —*Macbeth*

"I am sorry, Miss Barclay, but I can't work under these conditions!" Early the next morning, before Julia could even open up the household account books, Smithson, the head groom, came marching into her book room. He held Charlie Englehardt, whose face was scrunched in a pained grimace, firmly by the ear.

Julia regarded them through bleary eyes. She had managed only an hour of sleep, between running about in the woods with Marcus and then spending the rest of the night thinking about him. Being utterly confused about him.

After a quick breakfast of chocolate and toast in her chamber, she had hoped to make some progress on the accounts before she presented them to Marcus. Apparently, that was not to happen in the near future.

Thanks to Charlie, she must now placate an irate servant. Again.

Julia carefully set aside her pen and folded her

hands atop the account books. "What seems to be the trouble, Smithson?" she asked calmly.

"It is this . . . this *actor*, Miss Barclay! He knows nothing about horses."

That is why he is an actor and not an ostler, Julia thought. Aloud she said, "I told Charlie not to bother the animals, to just polish tack or muck out stalls; whatever you instructed him to do."

"Well, begging your pardon, miss, but he is not following those instructions."

Julia raised her brow sternly at Charlie, who promptly curled up in a little ball on the floor. "No?"

"No, miss. He told young Harry, the new stable lad, that he, Charlie, was to exercise his lordship's prized Beelzebub."

Julia gasped and shook her finger at Charlie. "Charlie Englehardt! I told you specifically not to go near any of the horses. Did I not?"

"Oh, Julia!" Charlie wailed, pulling his cap down to cover his eyes. "Lovely, merciful Julia! I only wanted to help. . . ."

Julia held up her hand, halting the flood of his words. Then she turned back to Smithson. "Was the horse harmed?"

"No, Miss Barclay, he—"

"Was the *horse* harmed?" cried Charlie. "Not a word about was *Charlie* harmed!"

Julia glared at him, causing him to whimper and draw his cap completely over his face. "Please, go on, Smithson," she said.

"Harry is looking after Beelzebub now. The poor horse isn't used to people jumping up on him bareback and yelling 'a horse, a horse, my kingdom for a horse.' "

Julia bit her lip to keep from laughing out loud at the vision of it all. She clutched her fingers together tighter and said, "I would imagine it is not something that happens to him every day."

"No, miss. It spooked him something awful. He threw this one off in a trice, and went crazy in the stable yard. We like to have never gotten him back in the stall. We were just lucky that his lordship chose another horse to ride out on this morning."

"Yes. Very lucky. Well, I can see that you are quite right, Smithson. It will never do for Charlie to stay in the stables frightening the horses."

A look of profound relief flashed across Smithson's weathered face. "Thank you, Miss Barclay."

"You may return to your duties."

Smithson bowed and departed in great haste, as if afraid she would change her mind and force him to take Charlie back to the stables if he tarried.

Charlie rolled about on the floor and moaned, " 'There is no creature loves me; and if I die no soul will pity me.' "

Julia sighed deeply. "Oh, do get up, Charlie, and cease that nonsense at once. I have no time for your caterwauling this morning."

"I only meant to help them, Julia, to make their day a little brighter. . . ."

"Just as you tried to brighten up the day of Mrs. Gilbert and Betty? No! Now you have very nearly cost me a head groom, as you nearly cost me a cook. What a fine mess we would have been in then. I am sending you to the head gardener, Charlie, and I vow that this is your last chance. You will have to go ahead of everyone else to Brighton if this does not work out well."

His face puckered in disgust. "The gardener!"

"Yes. He is to begin spreading the leavings from the stable on the flower beds today."

"But . . . but that is . . ."

"Yes, Charlie. That is manure. It helps the flowers grow in the spring. 'Our dungy earth alike feeds beast as man.'"

For once, Charlie Englehardt was outquoted.

Marcus returned from his ride late that afternoon. And he was not alone.

Julia watched from her book room window as he rode up the drive, accompanied by another gentleman, a rather portly man who sat his mount awkwardly. With them was a lady, elegant and very stylish in a blue-and-red riding habit designed *à la militaire*, with gold epaulets and gold buttons that dazzled in the sun. Her auburn hair was coiled smoothly beneath her blue tricorne hat, as if she had just left a hairdresser.

As Julia watched, the lady threw back her head and laughed at something Marcus said to her, revealing the swanlike length of her white throat.

· Lady Angela Fleming.

Julia felt a sourness stir deep in her belly. What was *she* doing here, laughing with Marcus, looking so cool and elegant and graceful? Julia had known she would have to see Lady Angela again one day;

she had just hoped it would not be quite so soon. And certainly not where Marcus would have a chance to compare Lady Angela's sophisticated perfection to Julia's more informal ways.

Marcus dismounted at the foot of the front steps and turned to assist Lady Angela. His hands almost spanned her tiny waist, and she smiled up at him charmingly as he placed her on her feet. She smoothed his cravat with her small, gloved hand before taking his arm and allowing him to lead her up the steps.

She swept one long, proprietary glance at the house, as if gauging changes she would like to make. Then she, Marcus, and the other man, whom Julia now recognized as Lady Angela's father, the Marquess of Belvoir, disappeared into the house.

Julia turned away from the window with a disgusted sigh. Marcus had looked so charmed, so dazzled as he gazed down at Lady Angela. But, then, he *was* a man, and like every other man in the neighborhood, he would be easily ruled by the Beauty.

Julia had thought, hoped, that he would be different. He had seemed very different last night, amid the ancient stones. How could he be snared by a charming smile and a stylish wardrobe?

Perhaps he had just been blinded by all the gold on her habit, Julia thought snidely.

She sighed again, knowing she would be summoned to the drawing room to play hostess at any moment. Somehow she would have to make herself more presentable than she had been the first time she met Lady Angela.

Julia went up to her bedroom and sat down at

her dressing table to brush the snarls from her curls, remembering that less than auspicious occasion.

It had been her very first ball after coming to live at Rosemount. She had been quite nervous, since it was her first proper ball. Oh, she had attended parties before, suppers and dances and card parties with her mother's friends. But never anything this grand. She wore her first grown-up ball gown and a lovely pearl necklace Gerald had given to her.

The very first thing she had done, there in the Flemings' grand ballroom, was to trip on the hem of that grown-up gown and spill punch down the skirt of Lady Angela's silver satin-and-gauze gown.

Thereafter, Lady Angela never missed an opportunity to make a cutting remark about Julia's appearance, intellect, or general demeanor.

Not that it had really mattered to Julia, except for the hurt it caused her mother. Julia had gathered her own small circle of anti-Fleming friends, and could, and often did, laugh about the Punch Incident.

It never mattered, that is, until now. Now that Marcus was here to hear Lady Angela's comments.

Julia laid down her brush and studied her reflection in the mirror. Her hair fell in its usual wild profusion of curls, always refusing to be tamed. It was ordinary brown, not gleaming auburn, or even guinea gold, as her mother's had been. Her eyes were only hazel, and not a fashionable blue. She was no Diamond.

But really, she was no troll either. Her nose was rather nice, and she had her mother's creamy complexion. If only she had some dazzling afternoon gowns, some stunning creations . . .

A sudden idea struck her. She rose from her dressing table and went out into the corridor.

Mary and Daphne were there, listlessly running feather dusters over picture frames and chatting aimlessly. They brightened when they saw Julia coming toward them.

"Where are you going, Jule?" asked Mary.

"Can we come with you, wherever it is?" said Daphne. "Dusting is only interesting for so long, you know."

"I am going to the attics," said Julia. "And yes, you can come with me. I could use your counsel."

"Ooh, the attics!" breathed Mary. "How exciting! What are you going to do there? Rattle chains so his lordship will think there's a ghost?"

Julia was so surprised at this that she quit walking. "Why would I want to do that?"

Mary and Daphne bumped into her, forcing her to move forward again. They turned up the narrow flight of stairs that led to the attics.

"It's not really such a bad idea," said Daphne. "We *could* rattle chains and drag furniture across the floor. Maybe moan a bit."

"But why would we want to do that?" Julia repeated.

"To make him think he is going insane, of course!" said Mary. "To drive him away from Rosemount so we can rehearse in peace."

"To send him fleeing in horror across the moors . . ." whispered Daphne.

Julia shook her head at them. "There are no moors nearby. Even if there were, I have no desire to send him fleeing across them." She unlocked the attic door and went inside. It was only dimly lit by the high, narrow windows, but it was still light enough to see the piles of trunks and crates.

"Then what are we doing up here?" asked Mary, gazing about at the jumble.

"Not devising a ghost." Julia walked over to the corner, where there was a group of trunks, all of them stamped in gold with the initials ABH—Anna Barclay Hadley. "We have guests this afternoon. So I need the most beautiful, the most dashing frock I can find." She opened up the nearest trunk to reveal an array of jewel-bright silks, satins, and muslins. "Who was ever more dashing than my mother?"

"Oh, yes!" Daphne stared down at the gowns, her visions of playing ghost vanishing before the allure of costuming. "Julia, we shall have you looking lovely in no time at all."

"Why, Miss Barclay. What a . . . sweet frock," Lady Angela said, her smile of welcome more of a lupine stretching of the lips over her teeth.

It *was* a sweet frock, as Julia well knew—more than sweet. And, if the rather stunned look on Marcus's face was any indication, he was aware of it, too.

"Thank you, Lady Angela. Your habit is also very . . . sweet. So much *gold*." Julia lowered herself onto a small chair opposite where the Flemings sat on a settee, careful not to crush her sapphire blue silk skirt or muss her white satin-slashed sleeves. "I do apologize for my delay in greeting you. Very remiss of me!"

Lady Angela's father, the Marquess of Belvoir,

merely grunted, being far too occupied with stuffing his mouth with almond cakes. Marcus, still looking dazed at Julia's sudden transformation to fine lady (at least Julia *hoped* that was why he looked dazed, and not from the long exposure to Lady Angela's charms), murmured, "Not at all, Miss Barclay. The tea has only just arrived."

"As you can see, I poured for everyone," said Lady Angela, gesturing toward the filled teacups arranged on the table. "So we were scarcely bereft, dear Miss Barclay. Marcus was just entertaining us with such delightful tales of his travels. Oh, I should call him Lord Ellston, should I not?" She smiled at Marcus, a genuine smile that made her blue eyes sparkle. "But we are such *old* friends that it is so difficult to be ridiculously formal."

As Julia poured out her own cup of tea, Lady Angela ostentatiously twitched her skirt aside, as if she feared tea would be spilled on it. Julia considered dropping in the lemon slice so hard that amber liquid would be sprayed out of the cup. Then she decided that she would never stoop to Lady Angela's petty level, and refrained. She smiled blandly as Lady Angela continued with her prattle.

"Do you remember, Marcus—Lord Ellston—that time we went fishing in your father's trout stream as children? You were such a horrid boy, you tried to put a fish in my pinafore pocket." She gave a trill of silvery laughter.

Julia grimaced and put a cake into her mouth so that it would be too occupied to say anything rude.

Marcus turned his attention from Julia, who looked so pretty in her new blue gown, to look at Lady

Angela in amazement. Of course he recalled that
trout incident. Angela had been trailing after him and
his friends all that morning, complaining about the
mud and threatening to go to his parents and tell
that he was fishing when he was meant to be at his
lessons. At last, fed up and goaded on by his friends,
Marcus had stuffed that fish into her pocket.

That had sent her fleeing across the fields, shrieking and screaming. It had earned him a scolding to
rival the one received for sliding down the banister.
But it had been worth it to free himself of Angela's
whining.

And now the tagalong child had grown into an
admittedly beautiful woman, one with a poise, style,
and family lineage that even his mother would have
approved of. He should be rejoicing that he would
not have to go to Town on his matrimonial search,
that a suitable choice had family lands that marched
with his own.

But somehow his attention kept wandering away
from Angela's chatter. He kept glancing at Julia, who
sat sipping her tea silently, a curious half smile on
her lips. He wondered what she was thinking; she
looked as if the entire scene had been set up in the
drawing room for her personal amusement. As if the
chattering Angela and her stout father, now stuffing
himself with all the salmon sandwiches on the tray,
were characters in a tableau.

They *were* rather amusing, he had to admit. He
almost laughed aloud at Angela's revisions of their
checkered childhood histories.

"Yes, it was so amusing!" she was saying about
the trout incident. She sighed as if in wistful nostal-

gia. "Father always did say that if he had been so fortunate as to have a son, he would have wanted him to be like you, Marcus. Did you not, Father?" Her voice rose sharply to get her father's attention.

"Eh?" The marquess looked up, startled, from his berry tart. "Oh, yes, of course, my dove."

"Yes," Angela continued. "Father always has been so fond of you, just as your *dear* mother was always saying how fond she was of me. I do believe she quite missed not having a daughter."

The only thing Marcus could recall his mother ever saying about Lady Angela was how useful it could be to have the Fleming lands attached to those of the Hadleys'. But she *had* been quite fond of that idea, so Marcus said, "Mother spoke very highly of you."

Angela smiled like the proverbial cat who swallowed the cream, and patted at her smooth hair. "Such a dear woman she was. The Harvest Fete has not been at all the same since she left us."

"But Lady Edgemere has always done a grand job with the Fete at Edgemere Park," Julia said quietly.

Angela looked at Julia sharply, as if surprised she was still there. "Well, yes, of course she has. But they have not been the same since the days they were held here at dear Rosemount." Angela sighed deeply again. "You were not in residence when the Fete was held here, Miss Barclay, but I am sure Marcus remembers those glorious days."

Marcus did remember the annual Harvest Fete. It was one of his most cherished memories of childhood, because it was the only time of year when his mother was too busy to scold him, or admonish him to behave like a proper little viscount.

The Harvest Fete had grown out of a medieval market that had once been in Little Dipping, and during the day of the Fete even the farmers and tenants were allowed into the gardens of Rosemount. There were tables and booths set up where they could buy fresh bread and cakes, roasted ears of sweet corn, or giant skewers of beef and vegetables. There were performers of all sorts, singers and jugglers. Above all, there was laughter and conversation. The hard work of the harvest was ended, and winter had yet to set in its icy hand.

At night there was a grand ball for the gentry. When Marcus had been on his wanderings, that was how he most often pictured Rosemount in his mind—lit up and glittering for a Harvest Fete ball.

"Certainly I remember the Harvest Fete," he said quietly. "So it is being held at Edgemere Park now?"

"Yes, but I hear that Lady Edgemere has said she does not want the bother of it anymore. I plan to offer to host it at Belvoir Abbey," Angela replied. "Father is so excited to host the Fete, are you not, Father?"

The marquess nodded around his mouthful of seedcake. "Whatever makes my dove happy."

Marcus somehow could not envision the merry Fete in the stark environs of Belvoir Abbey, with Angela to carefully orchestrate every moment until all the fun was gone from it. "I shall look forward to it," he lied.

"It will be coming up very soon," said Angela. "I must call on Lady Edgemere, to begin making the arrangements. It is the tradition for the last person who hosted the Fete to choose the new host, you know. But listen to me going on about the Fete, when the reason we came to call is to invite you to a party at the Abbey tomorrow evening."

"That is very kind of you," Marcus began, "but as I have only just arrived home again—"

Angela interrupted him with an airy wave of her hand. "Oh, it is not a ball or anything grand! It is only supper and cards with a few friends. Everyone is so eager to welcome you back, Marcus!" Her smiled dimmed as she looked at Julia. "You must come, too, of course, Miss Barclay."

"Of course," Julia murmured.

Marcus looked at Julia inquiringly. She merely raised her brow at him, as if to say, "*I* am not your social secretary. You must make up your own mind about the invitation."

He looked back at Lady Angela, who watched him expectantly. "We would be happy to attend, Lady Angela," he answered her. "Thank you for the invitation."

At that moment, the drawing room door was flung open, and the giant butler strode into the room.

"The cook has sent a special creation, my lord, in honor of your guests," he boomed. "I present the grand finale of the refreshments!"

Marcus half rose from his chair in alarm. He had no idea what was coming next, but he did know that whatever it was he ought to stop it.

Before he could do anything, the two footmen in their doublets and hose entered, bearing between them a large crystal bowl of what looked like frothy syllabub. They struck a dramatic pose next to the settee where the Flemings sat.

The butler strode over to the fireplace and lit the tip of a piece of kindling. Then he came back to where the footmen posed with the bowl.

"*Et voila!*" he cried dramatically, and touched the flame to the syllabub.

It ignited in a great "whoosh," causing Lady Angela to scream and leap to her feet.

As she did so, she jostled the arm of one of the footmen. He lost his balance and fell to the floor, dropping his end of the heavy bowl.

The sloshing liquid extinguished the fire, but a tidal wave of cream and port and lemon juice splashed all across Lady Angela's fashionable riding habit.

She gave a great wail and screamed out some very naughty words indeed. Something about cutting off the footmen's noses and feeding them to her horse.

With the Flemings gone at last, Julia crept up to her room and threw herself across her bed, rumpling the skirt of her mother's fine gown. Her head ached abominably, and she swore that she would retch if she had to drink another cup of tea—or syllabub—ever again.

The thought of a wretched evening with those people at their own home filled her with dread. She could have declined, of course, and probably should have after that disgraceful scene. But that seemed like conceding defeat. Defeat in what battle Julia was not sure, but defeat nonetheless.

She refused to wave the white flag to Lady Angela.

She might have to leave Rosemount soon, but she would not do it like some whipped puppy, shrinking away quietly. Well, not so quietly after the Syllabub Incident of today, which would surely supplant the Punch Incident in local folklore. By Jove, people might remember her as a clumsy ox, but they would remember her!

And she would make Marcus remember her, too. Then, some day, when he was shackled to Lady Angela and had ten bratty children, he would be sorry he let her go.

Julia sat up in the middle of the bed and reached up to free her hair from the pins that were gouging into her scalp. Whatever was she thinking, vowing to make Marcus remember her? Was she in love with him, then?

Perhaps she was, she admitted to herself. Just a tiny bit.

That was probably why she felt so jealous of silly Lady Angela, and why she felt such a wicked satisfaction at that ugly scene in the drawing room.

Julia giggled at the memory of Lady Angela covered in sticky syllabub, screaming like an Irish banshee while Abelard and Marcus ran about looking for towels. John and Ned had fled the room at the first opportunity, the cowards. They probably thought Lady Angela truly meant to feed their noses to her horse. And maybe she did, at that.

Julia laughed even harder to recall how the marquess had surreptitiously scraped some fluffy cream off his daughter's skirt and plopped it in his mouth.

She fell back to her pillows again, tears of helpless

mirth streaming down her cheeks. She kicked her heels in the velvet counterpane, and laughed and laughed.

Her stream of amusement was soon interrupted by a knock at her door. She sat up, wiping at her streaming eyes. "C-come in," she called.

It was her maid, Elly, looking rather like a frightened kitten. "Beg . . . begging your pardon, miss, but his lordship would like to see you in the library. At your convenience. But his lordship did make sure to mention that your convenience had best be soon."

So, it was time to pay the piper, was it? Well, Julia was willing to do so. He had played her such a merry tune this afternoon.

"I suppose the Flemings really are gone, then?" she said. She had stood on the front steps and watched them leave the house, but she thought it best to be sure.

Elly nodded silently, wide-eyed.

"And I suppose you heard the commotion in the drawing room?" How could anyone have failed to hear it? Lady Angela's invective had been quite loud enough to rise even to the attics.

Elly nodded again.

Julia had to struggle not to break into laughter again. Instead, she looked down at her dress and saw that rolling around in mirth had caused it to become quite wrinkled.

"Help me to change my gown, Elly," she said. "Then I suppose I must go down to speak to his lordship."

*   *   *

Marcus could not recall ever having such a splitting headache before.

He sat down at his desk in the library and buried his head in his hands. The house seemed to echo with silence after Lady Angela's storm of wrath.

Marcus thought he could safely say that nothing like that wild scene had ever been enacted in Rosemount's drawing room before. In his mother's day, such a thing would have been utterly unthinkable. Servants had always been orderly and unobtrusive under her sharp gaze. Guests had always departed unmolested, with their attire immaculately intact.

No doubt word of this debacle would soon spread throughout the neighborhood. Though Lady Angela had appeared mollified by his charming and effusive apologies before she left, he had seen the simmering anger in her pale blue eyes.

He should be angry, himself. He should be livid that the gracious rooms of Rosemount had been turned into a music hall spectacle. He should be furious with the servants, and with Julia, who had been frozen with shock at the scene, gaping at the screaming Lady Angela with wide eyes and unable to do anything to help.

He *should* be angry. But somehow he was not.

In fact, he had never been so diverted in all his life.

Marcus broke into laughter, and not just polite little chuckles. Great waves of mirth seemed to swell up from his chest and burst out in a tide of snorts and guffaws. He laughed until his ribs ached, until his cheeks cracked. He laughed until he had to lower his head to the desk and gasp for breath.

No comedy on the stage, no matter how brilliant,

could ever be funnier than the vision of the elegant Lady Angela covered in sticky syllabub, shrieking like a fishwife while her father scraped the cream off her skirt.

It *was* true that Marcus was vaguely considering making an offer for Lady Angela. She was, after all, quite suitable, and his mother would have approved. As a potential future Lady Ellston, then, he should have the respect not to laugh at her in her darkest hour. But he could not help himself. Even now he could feel another bubble of laughter rising up at the memory.

Then there was a soft knock at the door.

Marcus sat straight up and made a concerted effort to arrange his face in suitably severe lines. He straightened his rumpled cravat and pushed his hair back from his brow.

"Enter," he called.

Julia came into the room, her steps slow and her eyes downcast. A faint blush stained her cheeks, causing her freckles to stand out in golden relief. She had changed her silk gown for one of simple sprigged muslin, and her hair was once again twisted back in its usual knot at the nape of her neck.

She came to a halt several feet away from the desk. "You wished to see me?" she said.

"Yes. Please, do sit down, Julia," he answered, gesturing toward the chair across from him.

She sat down with obvious reluctance and carefully smoothed her skirt, still not looking directly at him. "I suppose you wish to discuss the, er, incident in the drawing room."

"An intelligent deduction," he said, steepling his fingers and bringing their tips to his lips to hide his grin. "It *is* the thing preying most on my mind at the moment."

She did look at him then, her hazel eyes wide. "It was not the fault of the servants! There is no need to sack them. It was I who asked that the syllabub be served."

She seemed quite desperate to get her point across. She leaned forward in her chair, and her fingers pleated nervously at the cloth of her skirt.

"Did you also ask that it be set alight?" he said.

"N-no. I did not even know that syllabub *could* be set alight."

"And did you ask that it be spilled on Lady Angela?"

"Of course not."

Marcus lowered his hands, folding them on the desk. "Julia, I think that we need to have an overdue discussion about the household staff."

Julia bit her lip. "The staff?"

"Yes. Was your mother perhaps running some sort of charity home for out-of-work actors?"

"Actors? Whatever gave you that idea?"

Marcus shrugged and sat back in his chair to watch, fascinated, as her blush deepened. "I do not know. They just seem to have a rather . . . dramatic bent."

Julia shook her head. "No. The staff is highly professional." *Not out of work at all.* "My mother had the highest esteem for them. I know that they may seem a bit eccentric on occasion . . ."

"On occasion!"

"But the meals are on time, the fires are lit, and the furniture is dusted. Are they not?"

"Yes. Of course."

"Then there is no difficulty. I *do* apologize for what happened to Lady Angela, and I will send her a note telling her so."

"That would be very good of you. I have already offered to pay for a replacement riding habit."

Julia's eyes, so wide before, narrowed. "Oh, did you? That was . . . generous."

Marcus smiled. "Perhaps it is not strictly proper, of course, but it seemed the only polite thing to do, after hers was ruined in my own drawing room."

"Polite, indeed," Julia murmured. "Well, if that was all you wanted to speak to me about . . ."

"It was."

"Then I should go and see how the cleaning of the drawing room is progressing."

"Yes, of course. I shall see you at supper, then."

Marcus waited until she was out of the room, with the door safely shut behind her, before bursting into laughter again.

He was going to buy that insufferable Lady Angela a riding habit? A gift of clothing, suitable only for one's intended?

Julia marched across the foyer, her arms crossed in indignation. Well, if *that* was the way the matrimonial wind was blowing, then Julia wished him happy of his chosen bride. Any man fool enough to choose a woman like Lady Angela Fleming deserved what he got.

She had just thought, or hoped, that Marcus was different.

But she had no time for foolish hopes now. She had other business to attend to.

She threw open the drawing room door.

They were all there. Daphne and Mary were sponging at the satin upholstery of the settee where Lady Angela had been sitting. John and Ned had rolled back the rug and were scrubbing at the parquet floor. Abelard was clearing the mashed remains of the refreshments—not that there was much left of them, after Lord Belvoir's onslaught. Even the young apprentice was put to work, scraping dried cream off of the rose-colored silk wallpaper.

"There you are, lass!" Abelard boomed. "Wasn't our performance this afternoon a triumph?"

Julia shut the door and leaned against it, folding her arms again. "Do you mean to say, Uncle Abby, that you did all of this on purpose?"

Abelard paused and stroked thoughtfully at his whiskers. "Well, no, lass, not on purpose. I mean, we *did* plan to set the syllabub alight. It was something Mary saw some Frenchy chef do once. But we never planned to spill it all on that harridan and her piggy father. That was the hand of fate."

"The hand of fate, ha! It was the hand of Abelard Douglas, and well you know it." Julia sat down on the one unscathed settee.

"What is wrong, Julia?" asked Daphne, leaving off her scrubbing to come and sit beside her. "Did his lordship give us the sack, then? Do we have to leave?"

"No, nothing that dire. But he did ask if my mother gave out-of-work actors staff positions out of charity."

"Out of work?" Abelard thundered. The very silk-covered walls shook. "Not one of Abelard's Ambling Players has been out of work for one day of their lives! We are the finest Shakespearean actors in all of England—"

"And of Scotland and Wales," Ned interjected.

Abelard slapped his hand against the marble mantel. "Damn right. Ireland, too! We are hailed throughout the kingdom."

"Uncle Abby, please!" Julia hissed. "What if Lord Ellston hears you?"

"I don't care if the bloody little Sassenach does hear me! *Let* him hear me. Let him come in here and challenge me himself. . . ."

"If he hears you, he will throw you all out for certain," Julia reminded him.

"Ah. Well." Abelard sank slowly down to sit on the nearest chair. "Perhaps the lad is not so very bad for an Englishman, after all."

Mary giggled. "You said he was a bloody little Sas—"

"That was before I really knew him," Abelard interrupted, giving her a stern look. "Remember what we talked about the other night? When the moon was full?"

"Oh, yes." Mary nodded, her blond curls bouncing. "I do remember now. Yes. Lord Ellston is not bad at all."

She dug her elbow into John's ribs, and he said, "No. Not bad at all. In fact, he's rather nice. Don't you think so, Julia?"

"You wouldn't have thought he was so nice if he *had* given you the sack," Julia murmured, completely mystified by their odd behavior. What had happened on the night of the full moon? "But as he has not, I think we should have more caution in the future. We should move the rehearsals to the dower house."

"Of course, lass," answered Abelard, his voice rather hoarse from his earlier tirade. "Whatever you think best. After all, this is *your* house."

Chapter Eleven

He plays o' the viol-de-gamboys,
and speaks three or four languages
word for word without book,
and hath all the good gifts of nature.
—*Twelfth Night*

"Oooh, Julia, look at this!" Daphne cried.

Julia looked up from the menus for the next week she was reviewing at the library desk. Marcus had gone out riding for the morning, so she had decided to use the library for her work while Daphne dusted the bookshelves.

Only Daphne was not doing very much dusting. Instead, she was perched atop her stepladder, her feather duster tucked beneath her arm, reading the books.

Julia happily put aside the menus; Mrs. Gilbert's crabbed handwriting was giving her a headache. "What is it, Daphne?"

"This book is *very* interesting. Someone has naughty taste indeed!" Daphne climbed down from the ladder and came to put the book on the desk.

Julia leaned forward, curious, to see a pen-and-ink drawing of a rather large woman with pendulous breasts falling out of her gown, sitting astride an equally corpulent man.

She choked on a gasp of laughter and looked

quickly away. Then she peeked back at it. "Oh, my. They seem rather, er, athletic for such large people."

"Don't they, though?" Daphne said gleefully, rifling through the pages. "And there's more, too. See? I especially like this one with the monkey . . ."

"Daphne!" Julia reached out her hand and slammed the book shut. "Wherever did you find this?"

"It was shoved behind some volumes of Plato up there on the top shelf. I wonder whom it belonged to?" Daphne peeked at the flyleaf. "No name written here."

"That's hardly surprising. Who would admit to it? I'm sure it wasn't Gerald's."

"Maybe it belonged to his first wife?"

"Marcus's mother? I don't think so. Everyone says she was so perfectly proper."

"Those are the ones you have to watch out for." Then Daphne snapped her fingers. "I know! I bet it was Thompson's."

"The butler?" Julia giggled at an image of the rabbity little butler eagerly devouring naughty literature.

"Well, why not? He was just the sort to do it, if you ask me. With that dried-up wife of his . . ."

"Daphne!"

"Sorry, Julia. But it's true." Daphne picked up the book. "What should we do with this lovely little volume, then?"

"Put it back where we found it, I suppose. I'm not taking it to *my* room."

"You are probably right; best just to forget all about it. It would have been funny to show it to Mary, though."

Daphne went to put the book back behind the Plato, and Julia went back to her menus.

She had barely gotten past the first course of supper when Mary came flying through the door. Her curls were escaping from her starched cap every which way, and her cheeks glowed pink with excitement.

"Oh, Julia! The grandest coach is just coming up the drive," she gasped. "Come and see!"

"I hope it is not the Flemings again," Julia muttered, putting away the menus for good. "I don't think I could stomach them so near to luncheon."

"If it is them, we'll just make some more syllabub!" said Mary.

The three of them hurried over to the windows to watch as the large carriage, a dazzling red-and-yellow barouche drawn by a beautifully matched team of bays, came gliding up the drive. There was a crest on the door, but Julia could not make it out at that distance.

"It can't be those Flemings," said Daphne. "That carriage is far too elegant for their tastes. Did you see all that gold on Lady Angela's habit yesterday?"

"It's too small for Lord Belvoir's backside, too!" snickered Mary.

Daphne leaned closer to Julia and whispered, "He probably posed for the drawing in that book."

Julia covered her giggles with her hand and turned her attention back to the new arrival.

As they watched, Ned, dressed today in a bright blue doublet and emerald green hose, hurried out to the carriage to open the door and lower the steps.

A tall, older woman in a pink pelisse and an elaborate pink-and-red feathered hat stepped out. She paused to gaze up at the house fondly, adjusting the ermine muff on her arm.

"Lady Edgemere!" Julia exclaimed. "Whatever can she be doing here? She only calls every other Tuesday. And she must have bought a new carriage; the old one was a plain black."

After her came a gentleman, nearly as tall as she was. He wore a somber black coat and plain neck cloth, but this attire could not disguise his angelic blond handsomeness.

"Who is *that*?" breathed Mary.

"I think it's Apollo," said Daphne.

"It's only Mr. Elliott, the curate," answered Julia, snapping her fingers to bring them out of their dazed regard. "I have no idea why he and Lady Edgemere have come to call, but I must hurry and change my dress before they see me! Will you both come and help me?"

"We'd rather serve tea to your guest. *Guests*, that is," sighed Mary.

"You can do that later," Julia said impatiently. "For now, though, come upstairs and help me choose a dress."

"My dear Miss Barclay, please do forgive us for calling on you with no notice. I know it is not my Tuesday," Lady Edgemere said, floating across the drawing room on the cloud of her pink pelisse to kiss Julia's cheek. "We just happened to be nearby, you see, making a parish call, and I wanted to stop here. I have something very particular I would like to speak with you about. You remember Mr. Elliott, do you not?"

"Of course," Julia answered, rather dazed by the whirlwind of energy that was Lady Edgemere. Even at the age of sixty-something (she would never admit exactly what the something was) she put everyone else to shame. Julia always felt in need of a nap after her calls. "It is very good to see you again, Mr. Elliott."

The curate took her outstretched hand and bowed over it, lingering just an instant longer than was strictly proper. "It is very good to see *you* again, Miss Barclay. I believe we have not met since St. Anne's choir concert a fortnight ago."

"No, indeed. Won't you both please be seated? Shall I ring for some tea? Or perhaps you would care to stay for luncheon?"

"Tea would be lovely, my dear, but then we must fly." Lady Edgemere sat down on the settee, while Julia watched, praying that the satin was dry from its sponging the day before. "I mean to attend the card party at Belvoir Abbey tonight, and I must make myself presentable! I understand you are going to be there, as well? Your first outing since your dear mother's passing."

The Flemings' party! Julia had been trying to forget all about it, and had quite succeeded until now. "Yes, of course," she murmured.

"Which brings me to what I wanted to ask you. I saw Lady Angela in Little Dipping this morning."

Julia clutched at the gilded arms of her chair, trying to brace for what was surely coming. "Did you, Lady Edgemere?"

"Yes. As you know, I have hosted the Harvest Fete

at Edgemere Park for several years, but this year I am simply too tired for all the fuss. As the previous host, I have the honor of choosing my successor, and Lady Angela tells me she would like to have it at Belvoir Abbey."

Julia was puzzled. Whatever did the Fete have to do with the flaming syllabub? "Oh?"

"Yes. She is quite eager to host it, in fact. It is quite an honor in the neighborhood, and she, of course, knows this."

Mr. Elliott nodded in earnest agreement.

"I thought Lady Angela was already quite a renowned local hostess," Julia said tentatively, not sure where this conversation was leading.

Lady Edgemere shook her head. "Lady Angela does have an influence among the more . . . impressionable of our younger set, perhaps. She is pretty, and young people, young men in particular, are rather susceptible to a pretty face. Excepting our dear Mr. Elliott, of course."

Mr. Elliott, who had wandered over to examine one of the paintings on the wall, bowed in acknowledgment.

"But you see, Miss Barclay," Lady Edgemere continued, "I simply feel that the Abbey does not have the . . . proper facilities to give the Fete its full honor. If you know what I mean."

Julia nodded slowly. She *thought* she knew what Lady Edgemere was saying—that Lady Angela did not deserve the honor of hosting the Fete.

"Therefore, Miss Barclay, I would like to ask you to host the Fete here at Rosemount. With Marcus's permission, of course."

Julia stared at Lady Edgemere, wondering if her hearing was failing her. She, to host the Harvest Fete? Why, she had never so much as hosted her own supper party before; she had only helped her mother. "Lady Edgemere, it is so kind of you to think of me. But I fear . . ."

Lady Edgemere held up her hand in an imperious, silencing gesture. "I know that it is a very large task, my dear, and I am prepared to help you in every way. As is Mr. Elliott. Are you not, Mr. Elliott?"

"In every way I can, Miss Barclay," Mr. Elliott answered earnestly.

Julia looked at Lady Edgemere in suspicion. "I thought, Lady Edgemere, that you said you were too tired for the Fete this year."

Lady Edgemere's faded blue eyes sparkled. "Too tired to have it at Edgemere Park, my dear. Never too tired to help a friend."

Julia considered this. Organizing the Fete would be a large task. Everyone in the neighborhood, gentry and farmers alike, attended. And then there was the grand ball in the evening. A large task, yes, but Julia could not resist the thought of the look on Lady Angela's face when she heard that she, Julia Barclay, was to host the Fete.

She smiled. "I would be happy to do it, Lady Edgemere."

Lady Edgemere laughed and clapped her hands in glee. "Excellent! It will be the finest Fete ever. It was always meant to be here at Rosemount; I don't know why your mother never wanted to host it. Mr. Elliott,

you must play us a celebration song on the pianoforte."

Julia looked over to see that Mr. Elliott was examining her mother's inlaid Venetian pianoforte. It had
not been played since her mother died, though Julia
always made sure it was still tuned. "Do you play,
Mr. Elliott?"

"A bit," he answered modestly. "You certainly
have a beautiful instrument here, Miss Barclay."

"A bit, he says!" snorted Lady Edgemere. "Don't
believe such self-effacement, Miss Barclay. He plays
like the veriest angel."

"Then do play for us, please, Mr. Elliott," Julia
beseeched. "I do not play at all, and I fear the instrument has been rather lonely of late."

"Do you sing, Miss Barclay?" Mr. Elliott asked,
sitting down on the matching bench and striking a
tentative note at the keys.

"Very little."

"Well, then, I shall only play if you agree to sing."

Julia glanced at Lady Edgemere, who said, "Oh,
yes, my dear, do. I should so love to hear you young
people make music for me. And here is the tea, as
well! Perfection."

Abelard came into the room then, carrying the tray
of tea and cakes. Julia gave him a sharp look, and he
nodded at her solemnly. There would be no flaming
syllabub today.

Lady Edgemere also gave him a long, penetrating
look, but Julia did not see, as she had risen to walk
over to the pianoforte.

"What would you like to sing?" Mr. Elliott asked.

"I fear my repertoire is limited. Do you know 'It Was a Lover and His Lass'?"

"Of course." Mr. Elliott nodded eagerly. "Everyone should know all the works of the Bard of Avon."

Julia smiled, liking the curate more and more. He struck up the lively tune, and she sang out: "It was a lover and his lass, with a hey and a ho and hey nonino . . ."

Marcus heard the music as soon as he came in the front door. It was sweet and lilting, filling the house with light.

The only music he ever remembered at Rosemount was the sad German *lieder* his mother had been so fond of playing, and that was nothing like this music. This music seemed to clear the very farthest corners of the house of shadows.

The two footmen, in their blue satin doublets, were dicing on the floor of the foyer. They leaped up when they spotted him, and came to take his hat and riding crop. The bells on their codpieces tinkled a light counterpoint to the music.

"Do we have guests?" Marcus asked them.

"Yes, my lord," answered the shorter of the two, the one with the plumed cap. "Lady Edgemere and Mr. Elliott, the curate."

That handsome curate he and Julia had glimpsed on the night of the full moon? Here, with Julia? He frowned. "How long have they been here?"

"About half an hour, my lord," said the taller footman. "Ab—Douglas has just taken in the tea."

Marcus strode across the foyer to the drawing

room. He knew that he really should go upstairs and change his clothes before greeting their guests; he was rather dusty. But he thought he would just peek in first, to see what was happening with Julia and the curate.

First he saw Lady Edgemere, with her elaborate pink-and-red feathered hat. She sat on the settee, smiling and nodding to the music.

Then he saw Julia. She was standing next to Mr. Elliott, who was playing at the pianoforte. And she was wearing her stylish sapphire blue silk dress again. Her hands fluttered as she sang, almost bringing them to rest on Mr. Elliott's shoulder. A beam of sunlight from the window alighted on them, bathing them in a celestial glow.

Julia sang out, "For love is crowned with the prime, in the spring time, the only pretty ring time, when birds do sing, hey ding a ding, ding, sweet lovers love the spring."

Mr. Elliott finished off the song with a light trill across the ivory keys. Then he and Julia smiled at each other in complete satisfaction.

A strange, sharp, unexpected anger at the sweet scene made Marcus break into slow applause, causing all three of them to turn their heads and look at him in surprise.

Mr. Elliott jumped up from the pianoforte and bowed politely, while Julia nervously smoothed her hair back into its neat coil.

Lady Edgemere smiled as if she had some great secret she refused to tell.

"Marcus, my dear!" she said, holding out her hand to him. "I am so glad you have arrived. I feared I would not see you on this visit. And you were just in time to hear the last of Miss Barclay and Mr. Elliott's song. Do they not sound delightful together?"

"Delightful," Marcus growled.

"Mr. Elliott is such a wonderful musician; he is wasted on merely playing for our choir practices."

"It is not often I have the honor of accompanying such a proficient voice," Mr. Elliott said modestly. "Miss Barclay could make any pianist sound wonderful."

The smile Julia gifted Mr. Elliott with was brilliant. Mr. Elliott offered her his arm to escort her back to the tea table. Her hand looked very small and dainty against the black sleeve.

Was she clinging to the man just a bit too hard? Marcus frowned.

"I did not recognize the song," he said, as Lady Edgemere handed him a cup of tea. "Was it Purcell?" Purcell was the only English composer he could think of.

"It was Shakespeare, you ignorant boy!" Lady Edgemere teased.

"From *As You Like It*," Mr. Elliott added solemnly, as if he were speaking of Scripture.

Julia gazed at him with admiring eyes. "Mr. Elliott took a First in Literature at Oxford."

"And he is also well versed in the Classics," added Lady Edgemere. "He speaks Latin like an ancient Roman." She gave Marcus a sly, sidelong glance.

Marcus found himself with a powerful longing to plant the perfect Mr. Elliott a facer, right on his perfect nose.

Instead, he took a long sip of the tea, wishing it were something a bit stronger. "Yes. Well. Anyway. I do apologize for not changing before greeting you, Aunt Fanny. When I heard that you were here, I was far too eager to see you."

"Yes. I am sure that is the reason." Lady Edgemere shoved a small china plate into his hand. "Here, my dear, eat your cake, and I will tell you why I have come to call."

Lady Edgemere waited until Mr. Elliott, Marcus, and Julia had walked ahead of her to the carriage before she took her muff from the waiting butler. She slid the fur over her arm and said, "Your name is Douglas, am I correct?"

He bowed. "Indeed it is, my lady."

"Well, Douglas, I have to tell you, I am not fooled by you for a moment."

He stood up very straight, his gaze startled. "My lady! Whatever do you mean?"

"I mean that if you are a butler, then I am the Queen of Sheba. I saw you act in *Macbeth* not two years ago at Drury Lane. It was a superb performance."

Abelard preened a bit, smoothing down his whiskers. "Thank you, my lady. The Scottish play *is* a particular favorite of mine."

"Yes, it is my favorite, too. You were far more convincing as the thane of Cawdor than you are as a butler. Are you fallen on such difficult times, then, that you are forced to go into service?"

Abelard glanced about nervously. "I am still on the stage, my lady. It is just that, well, things have become rather complicated. . . ."

"Say no more, my good man. Your secret, and I daresay Miss Barclay's, is safe with me."

She patted him on the arm, smiled, and swept out to her waiting carriage.

Chapter Twelve

> You were better speak first, and when
> you were gravelled for lack of matter,
> you might take occasion to kiss.
> —*As You Like It*

"I speak Arabic, you know."

Julia, who had been watching the countryside go
by outside the carriage window, eating up the miles
to Belvoir Abbey, looked across at Marcus in surprise. "You what?"

"Speak Arabic. Perhaps not like an ancient Roman,
like *some* people . . ."

"Of course not. Romans didn't speak Arabic, as far
as I know." Julia stared at him, utterly bewildered
by the conversation. What did Arabic and Romans
have to do with anything?

Then she remembered Lady Edgemere saying that
Mr. Elliott spoke perfect Latin—like an ancient
Roman. If Julia didn't know better, she would have
said that Marcus was jealous of Mr. Elliott.

But she did know better. Why would Marcus, who
was an earl, with all of Rosemount in his possession,
be jealous of a curate? Even one as handsome as
Mr. Elliott.

Julia shook her head. "Well, that is very nice that

you speak Arabic, Marcus. I will be sure to call on you if ever I meet any . . . Arabs."

Marcus nodded, seemingly satisfied with her answer.

Julia burrowed deeper into her cloak and went back to looking out the window. It was a chill autumn evening, perfect for curling up before the fire with a good book. She wished she were there now, cozy beside her bedroom grate, and not on her way to Belvoir Abbey.

She had tried to cry off, to plead a megrim, but Marcus would have none of it.

"Nonsense!" he had said when she tried to demure. "It must have been very dull for you these past few days, with only myself for company. A party is just what you need, Julia."

So here she was, dressed in another of her mother's gowns, hurtling through the darkness to what was sure to be a miserable evening.

She wondered vaguely if Lady Angela was planning on spilling wine on her at supper in retaliation.

All too soon, the lights of Belvoir Abbey came into view. The house looked exactly like what it had once been—a medieval abbey. It crouched in the middle of its park, long and low and dark. Pale orange light glowed from the mullioned windows, illuminating the shadows of the people passing behind them. A long row of carriages was lined up along the drive, waiting to deposit what appeared to be the entire county at the front door.

Julia could feel her palms begin to itch inside her gloves with apprehension. She reached up to straighten the fillet of ribbons and pearls that held her curls in place, and smoothed down her pale green silk skirt.

"You look lovely tonight, Julia," Marcus said quietly.

Her surprised gaze flew up to his. Was he teasing her? But no, his eyes were solemn and serious.

"Th-thank you," she stammered. "So do you. Look nice, I mean."

He smiled at her. "I will be the envy of every man here with you on my arm. Especially that curate. What was his name? Emerson?"

It sounded as if Marcus *was* jealous of Mr. Elliott, after all! Because of her? Surely not.

Julia had no time to examine these puzzling thoughts, though. A footman opened the carriage door then, and she was forced to alight, accept Marcus's outstretched arm, and walk on her suddenly unsteady legs into the Abbey's cavernous drawing room.

Most of the guests were already gathered there before supper, and they all turned to stare as Julia and Marcus entered the room. Or at least, so it seemed to Julia, who had quite hibernated after her mother's death and was no longer accustomed to such gatherings.

Her hand tightened on Marcus's arm as she looked about for a familiar face.

Lady Angela was seated prettily at the center of an admiring circle of young gentlemen, beneath a portrait of herself. Her father was speaking to Mr. Whitig next to the fire, popping peppermints into his mouth. Julia had no wish to speak with either of *them* until it was absolutely necessary.

Her gaze roved over the beautifully dressed cliques of people until she found what she sought. Lady Edgemere, in an eye-catching gown of burnt orange satin and a matching turban trimmed in tall yellow feathers, was standing across the room with Mr. Elliott and several others. She waved at Julia with her yellow feathered fan and leaned over to murmur in Mr. Elliott's ear. He, too, looked over at Julia and smiled in greeting.

Julia waved at them in return, and they began to thread their way across the room in her direction.

"Who are you waving at?" Marcus asked.

"Just Lady Edgemere. And Mr. Elliott. See, they are coming toward us." An imp of mischief prompted her to add, "Doesn't Mr. Elliott look so handsome in his blue coat?"

Marcus grunted in reply.

"There you two are!" Lady Edgemere cried, holding out her hand to Marcus and offering her wrinkled cheek for Julia to kiss. "I thought you were going to be too late for supper, and I did so particularly want to talk to you some more about the Harvest Fete." She leaned closer to Julia and whispered, "You just should have seen Lady Angela's face when I told her I had asked *you* to host the Fete!"

Julia giggled, but her laughter faded when she saw that Lady Angela had chosen just that moment to come up to them and lay her silk-gloved hand on Marcus's sleeve.

Her coterie of admirers trailed behind her, looking bereft at losing her presence.

"Lord Ellston," Lady Angela purred, "I am so glad

you have arrived, since you must escort me in to supper."

"It will be my most sincere pleasure, Lady Angela," Marcus answered.

Julia longed to frown sourly, to stomp her feet in vexation, but she forced her lips to turn upward instead, in a bright smile.

Then Lady Angela turned her attention to Julia. "And dear Miss Barclay," she said slowly, "such a very . . . charming gown, as usual. You must give me the name of your modiste; I am sure it must be someone local. Mrs. Porter in Little Dipping, perhaps? I detect a touch of the country in those sweet little bows." She daintily touched the puffed sleeve of her own sky blue lace gown. "All of my gowns come from London, of course."

Lady Edgemere gave her a disgusted look. "My dear Lady Angela, you must become more *au courant*. I detect the hand of Madame Auverge in Miss Barclay's ensemble. The famous Parisian couturier, you know. She once sewed for the Empress Josephine, and she has been quite exclusive since she emigrated to London. She would not even make a gown for Princess Esterhazy! Such a coup to have one of her creations, Miss Barclay."

It *had* been a coup for Julia's mother to get the gown, and Anna had been very proud of it, even though she had not had the chance to wear it in public. And now it was a coup for Julia, too, as she watched Lady Angela's coral lips compress into a tight line and a dull flush spread over her cheeks, clashing with her auburn hair.

Then Lady Angela looked back at Marcus and smiled sweetly. "If you will excuse us, Lady Edgemere, there is someone I would so like Lord Ellston to meet."

"Of course, my dear," Lady Edgemere replied. "Mr. Elliott and I were just going to discuss the Harvest Fete with Miss Barclay."

Lady Angela nodded curtly and moved away, tugging Marcus by the arm. He looked down at her attentively as she chatted and smiled up at him.

"Hmph," Lady Edgemere snorted. "If that boy falls for her simpers and giggles, then he is a fool."

Julia tore her gaze away from the departing couple to look at Lady Edgemere in surprise. "I thought she was just the sort of proper lady to be Countess of Ellston. Beautiful, of good family, accomplished. . . ." Julia was unable to go on; she feared she might choke on the words.

"Oh, she is all those things," Lady Edgemere agreed. "She is also a catty shrew."

"Lady Edgemere!" Julia and Mr. Elliott cried together.

"It is true. You needn't give me those shocked faces. You will find, my dears, that when you have reached the age I have, one of the few advantages is that one can say whatever one likes. Whatever the truth is that no one else dares say aloud. But we must not let her ruin our evening! Let us go sit down and talk of happier things. Like your butler, for instance, Miss Barclay . . ."

Throughout supper, Marcus found he could not concentrate on Lady Angela's chatter, or on the rather tough braised beef he was meant to be eating.

He kept glancing down the table, to where Julia sat next to Mr. Elliott.

She really did look lovely, like a spring leaf in her pale green silk gown. Her only jewelry was a single strand of pearls, but those, along with the brightness of her eyes, made the emeralds and rubies of the other ladies seem cheap and overdone.

And those bright eyes were now looking intently at Mr. Elliott as he spoke to her. She seemed quite spellbound by whatever the man was saying, nodding occasionally, or smiling softly.

Marcus wished with all his might that he could hear what they were talking about. What could be holding Julia's attention so deeply? But there were far too many people, too many conversations, between them, and Lady Angela's chatter was loud in his ear.

"I was just telling Father today how lovely it is to have my old childhood friend back!" she was saying now. "We did miss you so while you were gone. The neighborhood was quite bereft, and even everyone in Town spoke of how much you were missed. The Season was never the same without you."

"It is most gratifying to be missed," Marcus murmured, watching as Julia said something to Mr. Elliott.

"And so you were! Very much." Lady Angela glanced at him slyly. "But now that you are home again, you must have such plans for Rosemount, for the future."

Indeed, he did, and one of them was to double his excellent cook's wages, he thought, as he tried without success to cut his beef. "Of course."

"Yes. You will be wanting to take your place in Society."

"Perhaps."

"To start a family. I did tell Father . . ."

Whatever else she said was completely lost on Marcus, as he watched Julia laughing with Mr. Elliott.

Damn that curate! Why did he have to come and be the curate here, anyway? Weren't there needy parishes in Wales somewhere? And weren't men of the cloth supposed to be old and ugly?

". . . Do you not agree, Lord Ellston?" Lady Angela's words seemed to come to him from a hazy distance.

He tore his attention away from Julia's laughing face to look down at Lady Angela. "Er . . . of course," he said quickly.

She nodded with satisfaction and turned her attention back to her plate.

Marcus signaled to the footman to refill his drained wineglass.

"You seemed to have an enjoyable evening. Considering that you did not even want to go in the first place."

Julia, who had been softly humming "It Was a Lover and His Lass" to herself as she watched the miles back to Rosemount roll past the carriage window, smiled across at Marcus. He had seemed rather out of sorts ever since they departed the Abbey. Perhaps that was because he had been forced to share a card table with Lady Angela, her belching father, and Mr. Whitig, all of them notoriously bad card players?

Or perhaps it was because he was leaving Lady Angela behind, when he would much rather be in a carriage with *her* than with Julia.

Whatever it was, he looked quite grumpy.

"I did have a good time, thank you very much. I won at whist."

"Because you were partnered with Mr. Elliott?" Marcus growled.

"Mr. Elliott *is* an adroit card player. It may not be strictly proper, since he is a clergyman, but we quite roundly trounced Lady Edgemere and Lord Hallsby."

"And if we were to drive into a ditch just now, he could probably pull us out single-handedly," Marcus grumped. "If we were fortunate enough to have him come upon us, that is."

All right, now it was confirmed—Marcus *was* jealous of Mr. Elliott. The intriguing question was, why?

"What do you have against Mr. Elliott, Marcus?" she asked. "He is perfectly amiable."

"So amiable that you had to flirt with him all evening!" Marcus seemed to regret his words as soon as he said them. He turned rather gray in the faint light of the carriage lamps.

Julia was utterly aghast. "Flirting! Why, if anyone was flirting this evening, it was you and that Lady Angela. Mr. Elliott and I were simply having a pleasant conversation, while Lady Angela was practically sitting on your lap at the supper table. . . ."

Then, the next thing she knew, Marcus was sitting beside her, she was in his arms, and he was kissing her.

Her eyes widened in shock, then fluttered closed at the warm sensations that flooded through her veins like fine brandy. She looped her arms around his neck, burying her fingers in his soft hair, parting her lips in wonderful surprise at his seeking tongue.

She had never felt so wonderful, so alive, in all her life! She felt as if she could do anything, as long as his arms were around her. It was like magic. Like the wonder they had found in the midst of the ancient stones.

Then the carriage hit a rut in the road, and they were jolted apart.

Julia leaned back against the squabs, dazed, and watched Marcus's face as he stared back at her. He looked exactly how she felt—bewildered, overjoyed, and dismayed, all at the same time.

She touched her lower lip carefully, finding it damp and slightly swollen. "Marcus . . ." she said, then fell into silence. She was not sure what it was she had wanted to say.

"Julia," he murmured. "I am so sorry. What a dreadful mistake. Please forgive me."

A *mistake*? He was *sorry*? Julia almost gasped from the pain that lanced through her heart. She had just had one of the most beautiful moments of her life, and he was sorry.

She turned her back to him and stared sightlessly out the window. Why were they not home yet? The house, glowing with a welcoming light at the end of the drive, seemed so very far away.

"There is no need to be sorry, Marcus," she said stiffly.

"Of course there is, Julia! You are a lady, and I jumped on you like some ravening beast."

Oh, if only he had! "Please, think no more about it. I forgive you, if you like, but there is nothing to apologize for, really."

"Julia, I want to say . . ."

They came to a merciful halt before the front steps. As soon as Ned appeared to open the carriage door, Julia leaped out and ran through the house, stumbling in her heeled slippers. She did not stop until she was safely in her own room, and then she threw herself onto her bed and wept.

Chapter Thirteen

I love to cope him in these sullen fits,
For then he is full of matter.
                                    —*As You Like It*

It was very late indeed. Even the stars, earlier so bright in the night sky, had begun to fade. But Marcus knew that if he retired to his bed he would not sleep. So he stayed in the garden, sitting on a marble bench, smoking one of the thin, dark cigars he'd brought home from Egypt.

Staring up at the light in Julia's window.

Apparently, she could not sleep, either. Her bedroom light had been burning for hours.

Marcus started several times to get up and throw some pebbles at her window, just as he had on the night of the full moon. He wanted her to come to the garden, to sit beside him and talk with him. He wanted to hold her in his arms, to bury his face in her soft hair, to pour out to her all his regrets of that evening.

For he had so many regrets—a hundred at least. He regretted his ridiculous jealousy of Mr. Elliott; he regretted the childish temper he'd displayed because of that jealousy. Above all, he regretted kissing her.

Not that it had been unpleasant—far from it. It had

been the sweetest, richest kiss he had ever tasted. Julia fit in his arms, against his body, as if she had been designed to be there. At the merest touch of their lips, passion welled up between them like an irresistible, irrefutable force. One that had taken all his might to resist.

Marcus muttered a soft curse, and took a long, steadying pull on his cigar.

He was trying very hard to be honorable. He had played the prodigal son for too long; now he wanted to do what his family had always expected of him. To bring honor to the Hadley name once more.

A woman like Lady Angela Fleming was just what the *ton* would expect for a Countess of Ellston. He *should* marry her, no matter how sweet Julia Barclay's kiss was.

He had condemned his father for loving an actress; how could he, Marcus, be such a hypocrite as to do the same with that actress's daughter?

Marcus pressed his hand to his aching head, more confused than he had ever been before in his life. He wanted to do the right thing. But how could he know what that right thing was?

Then Julia appeared at her window. She stood there for one moment, looking like a true angel in her white nightdress, lit by the glow of candlelight. She looked out at the garden as she twisted her hair into one long plait, and Marcus saw all his own confusion and pain reflected on her face.

Then she closed the curtains and was gone to him. He was left alone in the darkness.

*   *   *

The next few days passed quietly and uneventfully. Julia found that she and Marcus could be polite, even cordial, when they met at breakfast or supper. But their earlier easy conversation was gone. Marcus seldom smiled, and he never joked. There were no more quiet after-supper talks in the library, no walks in the garden.

Even the actors were rather subdued, going about their servants' "duties" silently and then slipping off to the dower house to rehearse. Julia became very aware that all too soon they would be gone, and she would have to decide about her own future. Already Rosemount seemed less the sunny haven of laughter it had been in the last few days, and more the echoing sepulchre it had been after Anna and Gerald died.

At night, Julia would lie awake in her bed, clutching her turquoise scarab in her hand. If she could just find a way for her and Marcus to talk about the dark cloud that sat between them, that kiss. Perhaps if they could talk about it, it would cease to seem so momentous, so all-changing. Or at least she could quit brooding about it.

But she was not brave enough to mention it. She doubted she could even say the word "kiss" in front of him.

So it went on, the silence, growing heavier between them.

During the day, however, she had little time to brood. She was far too busy planning the Harvest Fete.

Every afternoon she went to Edgemere Park or Lady Edgemere came to Rosemount. Julia and Lady

Edgemere made visits to all the tenants' cottages and farmers' manors to invite them to the Fete and ask them to bring food or handiwork to sell. They carefully made guest lists for the ball, penned the invitations, and planned the decorations and the refreshments.

More often than not, Mr. Elliott would be there, as well. He accompanied them on their calls and made suggestions about the music for the ball. He was very attentive and unfailingly cheerful.

Unlike *some* men, such as Marcus Hadley for instance. He could certainly use a modicum of Mr. Elliott's easy charm these days.

"Was that Mr. Elliott *again*?" Marcus came into the drawing room, still dressed in his riding buckskins, and flopped down into a satin chair. He propped his booted feet on the low table, next to some of Julia's lists for the Fete.

Julia glanced up from the list she was perusing. "Yes, it was. He and Lady Edgemere and I were drawing up the final plans for the placement of the food booths. The workmen are coming to set them up tomorrow afternoon. If that is quite all right?" She reached out and nudged his foot with her pencil. "And you are getting dirt on my papers, Marcus."

Marcus removed his feet from the table and placed them solidly on the carpet. "I would wager that *Mr. Elliott* is far too much the perfect gentleman to ever track dirt into the house."

"Indeed he is. Most fastidious." Julia blushed a bit when she recalled what the perfect gentleman had told her, quickly, quietly, before he left that day. "I have something I would like to discuss with you soon, Miss Barclay. Something of great importance to both our futures."

Perhaps he would soon ask her to marry him. He had certainly been quite attentive these past few days.

But Julia could not say that to Marcus. Somehow, the mention of Mr. Elliott's name always caused Marcus to scowl.

So instead she said, "And where were you off to today? The attorney's offices in Little Dipping?"

"No, I paid a call at Belvoir Abbey," he said carelessly, flicking at a bit of dust on his gray tweed jacket.

Julia felt a stab of quick pain in the region of her heart. She lowered her eyes back to her list. "I trust all was quite well there."

"Quite. Lord Belvoir and Lady Angela send you their regards."

"I am sure they do." Julia quickly gathered up her papers, busily straightening them into a neat pile. The drawing room suddenly felt airless; she longed for escape. "Well, if there is nothing else you wanted to discuss, I must go change my dress. We are dining at the vicarage tonight, remember? Lady Edgemere and Mr. Elliott will be there, and they wanted particularly to see you."

"Julia, wait." Marcus laid his hand briefly on her wrist, stilling her quick movements. "There *is* something I would like to speak with you about. I have been a coward not to mention it before, but now I see that I must."

When he removed his hand, Julia stared down at her wrist, certain he must have left a warm mark there. "Yes, Marcus? What is it?" she said. But she feared she already knew.

"Our kiss in the carriage," he answered swiftly, as if in a hurry to push the words out before he lost his courage. "I fear that you may have misunderstood when I said that it was a mistake. That you may have thought I meant it was a mistake because you are . . . less than a lady."

His words were rather garbled, but Julia understood them perfectly. "Is that not true?"

"No! Never. Julia, you are the finest, the kindest, lady I have ever known. *That* is why it was a mistake."

Julia was thoroughly confused. She had feared, in her late-night worries, that perhaps he had been shocked by her eager response to his kiss. That he had thought her a wanton. But he was saying she was too much a lady.

Her head spun.

"I fear I do not rightly understand you," she said slowly.

"I was a cad to take advantage as I did," he answered. "Obviously, I have caused you pain by it. Things have not been the same between us these last few days."

"No. They have not."

"Well, I want to assure you that I will not lose control in that manner anymore. I want us to be friends again, Julia. I *need* us to be friends. Can we be?"

She slowly raised her eyes to search his face. He

looked so stricken, like a little boy who had been caught in some mischief and was deeply remorseful.

She wanted to throw her arms around him, to kiss his brow, to reassure him. And then, heaven help her, she wanted those kisses to turn heated, like the one in the carriage; she wanted to tumble with him to the carpet, to feel once again that intoxicating warmth in her veins.

But, being the perfect lady he thought her, she did not.

"Of course we are friends, Marcus," she said. "Always."

He smiled in relief. "Good. Then will you walk with me in the garden for a while?"

Julia glanced at the clock on the mantel. "The supper at the vicarage . . ."

"Only for a brief while. Surely your curate cannot be that impatient!"

"Very well. Only for a while."

Marcus was utterly fascinated by the myriad colors the sunlight picked out in Julia's hair. She had left her bonnet behind, and he could see the glow of chestnuts and reds and buttery yellows, all the autumn colors, as she walked beside him. The fringes of her Indian shawl brushed against his hand, releasing her lavender scent from its cashmere folds.

He had almost forgotten his careful new plan, concocted during his ride home from Belvoir Abbey, to treat Julia as a friend only. To be respectful of her. Every time he saw her he wanted so much to kiss her.

They could not go on living under the same roof for much longer or he *would* forget his plans, his resolutions. He had to persuade her to go to his cousin in London, or his aunt in Bath. Or he would go insane with trying to be a gentleman.

But maybe she was making plans of her own. Plans that involved the handsome curate, who always seemed to be at Rosemount these days.

"Mr. Elliott has become quite a regular visitor," he said carefully.

"Yes," Julia answered. "He has been so helpful to Lady Edgemere and myself concerning the Fete."

Marcus shook his head. "What I meant was, he seems very attentive to *you*. Personally."

Julia stopped walking and looked up at him. He could read nothing in her cool, bland hazel gaze.

"Mr. Elliott and I have a great deal in common," she said. "We both enjoy music and books. He has a great knowledge of Shakespeare."

Whereas he, Marcus, knew only "To be or not to be," which his boyhood tutor had forced him to learn. "Has Mr. Elliott been in the neighborhood very long?"

"Not very. Only about four months. But I have enjoyed every encounter I have had with him."

Every encounter? "So you like him? You share a friendship with him?"

"Yes," she said with a small, incomprehensible laugh. "Just as you enjoy a friendship with Lady Angela Fleming, Marcus."

"I did not mean that . . ." he began, but she had hurried ahead of him on the path, turning a corner and forcing him to pick up his pace to keep up.

He almost ran into her as he swung around the corner; she stood statue still in the middle of the path, looking at a strange sight.

Marcus himself could not help but gape.

A gardener worked in one of the flower beds, yet he was the strangest gardener Marcus had ever encountered. The man wore a huge straw hat that was pointed like some Oriental pagoda, and a flowing, Renaissance-style robe. He was singing some rather bawdy tune as he worked.

And he was busily digging up bulbs and placing them in a neat pile at the edge of the bed. Bulbs that had been imported from Holland at great expense, as Marcus knew from the bill he had looked at not two days before.

"Who is that man?" he asked Julia in a low, outraged voice. "And why is he digging up bulbs that were just planted?"

"He is . . . one of the under gardeners," Julia answered, so quietly that Marcus had to bend close to hear her.

"Well, I am going to speak to him about it right now! Those bulbs are very expensive."

"No, Marcus, please!" Julia laid her hand on his arm, stopping him in his tracks. "I will speak to him. You wait here."

"Julia, it should not fall on you to take the servants to task."

She gave him a little smile. "I have been doing that since my mother died. Just leave everything to me."

Julia marched up to Charlie Englehardt, her fists planted on her hips. "Charlie, whatever do you think you are doing?" she said sternly.

Charlie looked up at her, all wide-eyed innocence. "Why, I am gardening, Julia. Just as you asked me to."

"I never asked you to dig up those new tulip bulbs from Holland! Those have just been planted."

"Is that what these little things are?" Charlie held up one of the white bulbs and gazed at it in wonder. "I thought they were vegetables. I was going to take a basket of them in to the cook, as an apology."

"I hardly think Lord Ellston would appreciate being served a tulip pie." She looked back at Marcus, who was watching them with a suspicious frown on his face. She gave him a little wave. "He already suspects something is odd about the staff. Do you want to ruin everything, when we have come so far?"

"No, Julia! And I don't want to go back to the stables, either."

"Then replace the bulbs, please, just as you found them. And look sharp about it."

She gave one more stern nod, then went back to where Marcus waited. "Everything is fine now," she said, taking his arm and steering him back to the main pathway. "It was all just a misunderstanding."

Chapter Fourteen

It is as easy to count atomies as to resolve
the propositions of a lover.

—*As You Like It*

"Well, now, Lord Ellston," Mr. Whitig said, scooping
up the last of the excellent fillet of sole from his plate
and starting on the newly served dessert, "I must
say I will certainly be happy to see the Harvest Fete
come to completion! I have scarce seen my curate
these last few days; he is always at Rosemount, going
over the arrangements for the Fete." He gave said
curate a jocular grin. "But I think we all know what
his true purpose there is."

Marcus's eyes narrowed as he watched Mr. Elliott
blush. Why would the man blush if all he was doing
was concocting lists? There must be more to Mr.
Whitig's words.

Marcus had known it all along. The blighted curate
was after Julia. The question was, did Julia mind
the chasing?

He glanced over at her, but she looked calm and
tranquil, as cool as the ice blue of her dress. Her face
gave away none of her thoughts. She smiled at Mr.
Whitig and said, "I fear that is entirely my fault, Mr.

Whitig. It is an enormous task to prepare for the Fete, and Mr. Elliott has been an invaluable help."

"Indeed he has," added Lady Edgemere, who, along with Mrs. Whitig, rounded out their small supper party. "St. Anne's has such a treasure in Mr. Elliott." She winked at Marcus over the rim of her wineglass, as if she knew what he was thinking and found it quite amusing.

Marcus reached quickly for his own wine, taking a long sip to cover his discomposure.

"Oh, yes, a treasure," said Mr. Whitig, sitting back from his plate, satisfied at last. "Mr. Elliott has the choir well in hand now, where before they could scarce sing in unison, and he is gathering funds to restore the stained-glass windows."

"Assisting us with the Fete can only help him in that endeavor," said Lady Edgemere. "By the time we are finished, we will have spoken to every family in the neighborhood. I am sure a small word to them about the windows will not come amiss."

Mr. Whitig laughed. "Lady Edgemere, I do admire the way your mind works!"

"Thank you, Mr. Whitig."

"Shall we all repair to our little drawing room for some sherry?" asked the plump little Mrs. Whitig. "And perhaps Mr. Elliott and Miss Barclay would favor us with some music? Lady Edgemere told me she has never heard anything so sweet as your duet."

Mr. Elliott glanced shyly at Julia and said, "I would be deeply honored to play accompaniment for Miss Barclay again."

I just wager you would, Marcus thought sourly. But he just smiled and said, "What a rare treat, indeed."

Julia looked at him suspiciously. His smile widened.

"What a lovely evening," Julia remarked, as they turned out of the vicarage gate onto the road in Marcus's light curricle. It was such a warm autumn night that they had left the closed carriage at home. That was the agreed-upon excuse, anyway; neither of them wanted to speak again of what had happened the last time they were alone in the dark carriage. "I do so much prefer small parties, don't you, Marcus?"

"Mm-hmm," Marcus murmured.

"The conversation is so much more comfortable. And was Mr. Elliott's playing not exquisite?"

"He was too loud," Marcus said. "Your singing is much finer than his playing, but he was so noisy you could scarce be heard."

Julia looked at him in surprise. "Why, Marcus, did you just compliment my singing?"

"Of course. You have a beautiful voice."

"How very sweet of you! No one ever complimented my singing before."

Now it was Marcus's turn to be surprised. "How could they not?"

"Well, my mother had a glorious voice, you see. While I had lessons when I was young, and Mother often made me sing at parties, people would always say, 'Oh, she has a sweet voice, but she will never be her mother's equal.'"

Marcus snorted. "That is ridiculous."

"Indeed it was. Almost as ridiculous as your unfounded dislike of Mr. Elliott."

"Why do you think I dislike the man?"

"Oh, I do not know. I believe it must be the way your lips pinch together when you look at him. Or the way your nostrils flare, as if you were smelling something foul. Or . . ."

"Enough! All right, perhaps Mr. Elliott and I will never be cronies. But I am sure he is very worthy in his profession."

"He is very worthy." Julia leaned back against the seat with a sigh, and looked out contentedly at the night. "Is it not beautiful tonight? The perfect autumn evening. I only hope this weather stays until after the Fete."

"Yes." Marcus turned the horses down the lane that led eventually to Rosemount. "May I ask you something about the Fete, Julia?"

"Of course."

"Why, after I left, was it still held at Edgemere Park and not at Rosemount? It had been at Rosemount for as long as I can remember. Did your mother not wish to host it?"

Julia hesitated for a moment, toying with the fringes of her Indian cashmere shawl. Then she said, "The truth is, Marcus, that my mother felt too . . . well, too insecure to host the Fete."

"Your mother? The famous Anna Barclay? Insecure?"

"I know it sounds ridiculous, and Gerald told her that many times. My mother was supremely confident in her art; she was a fine actress, and she knew it. She worked hard for it. Being a countess was very new to her. She wanted to be as perfect at it as she was on the stage. The Fete was simply far too much for her that first year, and after, when she felt more sure of herself, it was just easier to go on having the Fete at Edgemere Park. Mother hosted a large Christmas ball instead.''

Marcus mulled over this in silence. When he had been gone from Rosemount, he had often imagined his father's wife flaunting her new position, redecorating Rosemount, giving lavish balls, and having her wild friends to stay for long house parties.

But now he knew that he had been very wrong. In everything around him, in the elegant furnishings at Rosemount, in the way Lady Edgemere spoke of her, and most especially in her refined daughter, Marcus saw how badly he had misjudged Anna Barclay. She had not been vulgar and grasping; she had been a true lady. Just like her daughter.

His father had known that. He had seen the true beauty of Anna and Julia, whereas he, Marcus, had been nothing but a blind, snobbish fool.

Never had he felt more ashamed than he did in that moment.

He looked over at Julia, who was watching him with a puzzled air. How he longed to put his arms around her, to beg her forgiveness for the foolish, callow boy he had been! If he could only have those four years back, how differently he would do everything.

But that was impossible, and well he knew it. All he had was the present moment.

He drew up on the reins, bringing them to a standstill in the middle of the lane.

"Why are we stopping?" Julia asked. "Is something amiss?"

"Would you walk with me, Julia?" he said, his voice rather hoarse.

"What do you mean? Get down right here and walk?" Julia looked as if she rather feared he had lost his mind.

"If we go down that pathway there, we could walk to the stones," he answered. "The carriage will be fine for a while, if we leave it in the shadows."

"Marcus . . ."

"Please, Julia. Walk with me to the stones."

She nodded slowly. "All right. Yes."

Julia led the way again as they made their way to the stone circle. The moonlight was much dimmer than it had been on their last visit, but she knew the way by rote. She turned left at the special oak tree, and they were in the clearing.

She walked into the middle of the circle and looked back over her shoulder at Marcus. He looked more solemn than she had ever seen him, more haunted.

If anyone had ever had need of the magic of the stones, it was Marcus. Yet she had no idea why that could be. He had been rather quiet at supper, true, but he had seemed to have a pleasant time. Surely this new melancholy had to do with something other than a petty jealousy of Mr. Elliott.

Julia wanted to shake Marcus, to demand that he tell her what was wrong and how she could make it better. She knew that would never work, though, so she just sat down on the flat rock and watched him as he paced the perimeter of the stones.

Finally, he came and stood beside her.

"Would you tell me how my father met your mother?" he said quietly.

Julia stared up at him, certain she had not heard him right. Why would he, who had quarreled so violently with Gerald about her mother, want to know that?

Her first instinct was to not say anything, to hug her precious memories of Gerald and her mother close to her. They were more valuable than rubies to her, all she had left. Selfishly, she wanted to guard them.

Then Marcus said, "I know why you hesitate, Julia, and I do not blame you for it. But I promise I mean no mockery at all. I truly want to know."

Julia studied him carefully. All she saw in his eyes was sincerity.

She slid over on the rock, and he sat down beside her. "Gerald came to see Mother perform in London, in *The Merchant of Venice*," she began.

"Like the portrait in the drawing room."

"Yes. He came every night for a week, and sent her a bouquet and a note each of those nights. Mother thought he was just like all the others who sent her letters and gifts, and she refused to meet him." Julia looked at Marcus rather defensively. "She *always* refused to meet any of them. There was never any man in her life after my father died."

"I know that now, Julia. So how did my father finally catch her attention?"

"He sent her one last letter, a very long one, in which he told her why he found her Portia so very superior to every other actress's he had ever seen. He had a great knowledge of Shakespeare, you know."

"Yes." Marcus smiled faintly. "He always tried to impart it to me, with not much success, I fear. He dazzled your mother with his love of the Bard, did he?"

"Well, perhaps dazzled is the wrong word. But it won him a meeting. He came to tea at our house, and if he was surprised to find that he had to share the time with my mother with her young daughter, he gave no indication. He talked with both of us for a very long time, about so many things. Gerald was so charming. Just like his son!"

Marcus laughed. "My father's charm far exceeded any I might have."

"Not at all. You are very much like your father. Anyway, after that he was a regular caller. He took us driving in the park and to Gunter's for ices. One night, when my mother did not have to be on the stage, he even took us to Vauxhall to see the fireworks. After only a month, he asked my mother to marry him, and she said yes." Julia turned to look steadily at Marcus. "She loved your father very much, and she made him happy during their marriage. Just as he made her happy."

"I am glad, Julia. More than I can express, I am glad that they found happiness together." He took her hand in his and held it very tightly. "I cannot apologize to your mother, for she is beyond me. So I must beg forgiveness of you, Julia, on her behalf."

Julia stared at him, shocked. "Oh, Marcus, I scarce know what to say."

"You can say you forgive me," he said hopefully.

"You had my forgiveness a long time ago. You had my mother's, too. Nobody was ever more understanding of human foibles than she. She had seen it all in the plays she performed, and she said you were only young and confused. That you only needed to find your own way, and she was confident that you would. And so you have!"

Had he? Marcus was not so certain. But it did feel as if a great weight had been lifted from his heart. "Thank you, Julia, for sharing this with me."

"Thank *you*, Marcus, for allowing me to tell you. I miss them so much. Having someone to share them with seems to bring them back to me."

"Yes. To me as well." He looked about them, at the tranquil stones. "I have kept you far too late. You must be cold and tired."

Julia rubbed at her suddenly throbbing temple. "Very tired, indeed." But very happy, as well.

Chapter Fifteen

Come, woo me, woo me; for now I am in a
holiday humor, and like enough to consent.
—*As You Like It*

The day of the Harvest Fete dawned bright and
warm, with all the colors of the autumn trees at the
peak of their brilliant reds and golds. A perfect day
for merriment.

Everyone arrived early to fill the booths with food
and handiwork, and by noon it seemed the entire
county filled Rosemount's grounds. The scent of
roasted corn and meats and baked cakes hung in the
warm air. Families gathered on blankets beneath the
shade of the trees for picnics, while young couples
could be seen slipping in and out of the summerhouse for quick kisses. Little children, their faces
sticky with jam and toffee, watched the jugglers and
musicians in awe.

Julia strolled among all the chatter and laughter,
surveying the bright scene with great satisfaction.
She had been awake very late the night before, putting all the finishing touches in place. It seemed
worth every sleepless moment now, as she looked
about at all the excited, happy faces.

Rosemount was at last coming to life again, after

its long mourning. Just as Julia's heart had felt alive again these last days with Marcus.

She turned at the end of the booth-lined pathway to look back at the house. All the windows were thrown open, with long silk banners hanging from their sills that dressed the gray stone in crimson and yellow gaiety. Mary and Daphne, who had shed their black housemaids' frocks for their own dresses of pink and yellow muslin, had organized a game of blindman's buff for the children on the terrace. They were using Ned for their first victim, and he stumbled about comically, grabbing for the gleefully shrieking children.

Julia smiled as she watched them. This was what Rosemount needed—life, and children.

And, oh, how she wished they could be *her* children. She could just see them here, a sturdy little boy and a curly haired little girl, running about, laughing, and making their sweet faces sticky with toffee. They would wave to her and call out, "Mama, Mama, watch me!" as they dashed off to some mischief.

Then her daydream shifted, and she saw their father grab them up in a hug and kiss their plump cheeks as they giggled and squirmed. In her imagination, he turned to her, and it was—Marcus.

The children had his dark, silky curls and her hazel eyes.

Julia gasped at the stab of longing, and the fragile bubble of her vision burst in the face of reality. She stood alone, among a great crowd of happy families. And Marcus was strolling among the flower beds with Lady Angela Fleming.

Julia could see them from where she stood, could see Lady Angela's gloved hand on his arm and the silk roses on her bonnet bobbing near his shoulder. She might as well dream of going to the moon as of having children with Marcus. As of having Rosemount for her home forever, and raising a family there.

She felt tears prickling at her lashes and wiped at them impatiently with the back of her hand. This was no time for such maudlin thoughts! This was to be a day of celebration, of enjoyment. She refused to ruin anyone's fun, even her own, on such a day.

So she straightened her wide-brimmed, ribbon-trimmed straw hat and walked on to survey the rest of the crowd.

On the next row of booths, she encountered Mr. Elliott, who broke away from the giggling gaggles of girls that surrounded him and fell into step with Julia.

"What a successful Fete it has been, Miss Barclay!" he said. "It is my first one here, of course, but several people have told me that it is the finest one they have ever attended."

"The day is not yet over, Mr. Elliott," Julia answered. "But I think we can safely say that, barring something like an unforeseen rainstorm, it will be a grand Fete."

"Indeed it will. Thanks to all your hard work, Miss Barclay."

"And yours, Mr. Elliott."

They strolled along for a while in companionable silence, occasionally stopping to chat with groups of people or to sample one of the booths' culinary wares. When they reached the little summerhouse, all the young couples fled, tossing guilty looks in the curate's direction.

"I sense that Mr. Whitig and myself will soon have many banns to read," Mr. Elliott commented as they sat down on one of the deserted benches.

Julia stretched her tired feet in her kid half boots, deeply grateful for the chance to sit. "I am certain you will. But if they wish to wed before winter comes, they had best hie themselves off to Gretna Green." As her mother and Gerald had. Julia smiled to recall their hasty but oddly sweet and romantic nuptials.

"Oh, no," Mr. Elliott said, shocked. "Surely they would want a proper, sanctioned wedding. Doesn't everyone?" He paused. "Don't you, Miss Barclay?"

"Want a proper wedding?" Of course she did. A lace veil, white rosebuds, a cake, and all the trimmings. That had to come before the curly haired children.

She shook her head as maudlin thoughts threatened again. "Certainly I want a proper wedding," she murmured. "One day."

Mr. Elliott leaned closer, his expression deeply earnest. "Miss Barclay, I told you the other day that there was something I wanted to speak with you about. I know that this is not the proper time, but may I call on you? Tomorrow, perhaps?"

Julia knew what he was asking. He had been so attentive throughout the planning for the Fete, and Mr. Elliott was much too respectable a man to pay such attention to just any woman. He had also commented several times on how sensible she was, how efficient, and what a good "helpmate" she would be for a man of the church.

She studied his earnest, handsome face carefully, trying to insert him into her daydreams of weddings and children.

He was quite good-looking; that was undeniable. And he had a good heart and was devoted to his work. If she married him, they would have an eminently respectable life together. They would never have a home as grand as Rosemount, of course, but very soon he would surely have his own living and there would be a comfortable vicarage. They could read Shakespeare together in the evenings; she would do good works in the parish.

It all seemed very cozy. But, despite his basic goodness, Mr. Elliott had no spark of humor about him. Their children would not giggle and make mischief, like the children in her vision, like she had herself as a child. They would solemnly work on their lessons and give her no trouble.

Was that really what she wanted for her life?

Then she looked back out over the garden and saw Marcus and Lady Angela walking there, sharing a ginger cake, laughing and talking.

She turned away from them, back to Mr. Elliott. He waited for her response, his calm eyes patient.

Well, the least she could do was hear the man out. "Very well," she said. "You may call on me one day next week."

*   *   *

"Psst, Abby! Look at that." Mary tugged at Abelard's sleeve, nearly causing him to spill the tray of lemon tarts he was offering to passersby.

"What is it, Mary?" he muttered out of the side of his mouth. "Can't you see I'm butlering?"

"But look over there! Beside the summerhouse."

Abelard looked—and almost dropped the tray anyway. Julia stood there, posed in a sweet scene with a gentleman who was just raising her hand to his lips for a kiss. The trouble was, it was the wrong gentleman. It was not Lord Ellston; it was Mr. Elliott, the curate.

"That obnoxious little minister," Abelard growled.

"He's not a minister yet. He's just the curate." Even though Mr. Elliott was too far away to see her, Mary patted the blond curls that had been disarranged by blindman's buff back into place. "It looks like we need a plan, if Julia and his lordship are going to be together. It would break poor Julia's heart to leave Rosemount."

"You are quite right, Mary," Abelard said slowly. "We do need a plan, and we need to put it in effect tonight, at the ball. Tell the others to meet at the dower house in an hour."

"You look so pretty, Miss Barclay." Elly sighed as she put the final touches on Julia's coiffure for the ball. "Just like an angel."

"Thank you, Elly," Julia said, trying not to squirm nervously on her dressing table bench. "Are you sure I shouldn't wear the green velvet, instead?"

"Oh, no, miss. This is perfect."

There had been no time to have a new gown made, and all of her mother's other dresses had already been seen in public, so Julia had just redone one of her own gowns. It was of white muslin, falling in classically simple lines from its high waist and rounded neckline.

Julia had removed the white frill of lace that used to trim that neckline and replaced it with turquoise satin ribbon. More of the ribbon encircled the waistline and threaded through her upswept hair. It was to match the turquoise scarab Marcus had given her, which hung on its new gold chain about her neck.

"There, now!" Elly stepped back to survey her handiwork. "You are all ready for the ball, miss."

Julia twisted her head about, examining the smooth chignon of her hair. For once, not a single curl escaped. "Elly, you are a miracle worker."

Elly blushed a bright pink. " 'Twas nothing, miss."

Mary came running through the door then, without so much as knocking. She wore her neat housemaid's black again, but her white apron was crooked and her cap lay askew. "Oh, Julia! You are wanted in the . . ." She broke off midword, staring at Julia with wide eyes. "You look beautiful."

Julia laughed. "You needn't sound so surprised! I am not such a ragamuffin as all that."

"Of course you are not. I have just never seen that gown before. And what is that around your neck? Some sort of blue bug?"

Julia touched the turquoise lightly, running her fingertip over the carving. "It is an Egyptian scarab. It brings good fortune."

"We could all use some of that these days." Then

Mary seemed to remember what she had come running into the room about in the first place. "Oh, you're wanted down in the wine cellar! There's some sort of emergency there."

Julia frowned. The very last thing she needed right before the Harvest Fete ball was an emergency with the wine. "What kind of emergency?"

Mary shrugged. "A wine emergency, I suppose. Or perhaps a sherry emergency. Abelard sent me to fetch you."

"Then I had best go see about it." Julia gathered up her gloves, her white lace fan, and her turquoise-colored silk shawl, before going downstairs to avert the "wine emergency."

"Lord Ellston," Abelard boomed, "I fear you are needed down in the wine cellar. There is an emergency."

Marcus had just finished dressing for the evening and was carefully placing his emerald-headed stickpin in his cravat when the butler interrupted him.

"An emergency?" he asked, puzzled. "In the wine cellar?"

"Yes, my lord."

"Can't you take care of it, Douglas? The guests will be arriving in little more than an hour."

"Oh, no, my lord. I fear only you can resolve this particular emergency. The entire midnight supper could depend on its successful resolution."

"Oh, well, in that case . . ." Marcus took his blue superfine coat from the chair where it lay and shrugged into it before going downstairs to see to the "emergency."

After Julia and Marcus were both safely dispatched to the wine cellar, Abelard and Mary met in the corridor.

"Julia has gone," Mary whispered furtively. "Is all in readiness?"

"Ned is waiting for the signal."

"Excellent!" Mary straightened her cap and pinched at her cheeks to give them some becoming pinkness. "I shall distract Mr. Elliott when he arrives, then."

"Hello?" Julia called out. Her voice echoed hollowly in the cavernous wine cellar. She stepped into the room tentatively, holding the hem of her skirt off the stone floor. Ever since she had been accidentally locked in one of her mother's small dressing rooms as a child, she had been wary of dark, closed spaces. "Abelard? Are you here?"

"Julia? Is that you?" Marcus stepped from behind a shelf of wine bottles at the far end of the cellar. He held a candle in one hand, and the flickering light illuminated his puzzled features.

"Marcus? Why are you here?"

"I was told there was some sort of emergency. That footman told me it was over here, behind this shelf."

"What footman?"

"The one who always wears the little plumed cap."

"Ned," Julia whispered.

"Why are *you* here, Julia?"

"I was also told there was an emergency."

"Were you? How odd. Well, there doesn't seem to be any emergency at all."

Of course there was not. There was only mischief-making actors.

Julia turned back toward the door at the same instant that it swung shut. There was the rusty creaking of a lock shooting home.

She ran over to the door, banging at the stout, iron-bound oak with her fists. "Let us out right this instant, Abelard! I know what you are trying to do, and if you do not let us out, you will be very, very sorry."

"Julia? Who are you shouting at? What is the matter?" Marcus hurried down the length of the cellar to her side. He stared dumbly at the closed door. "Why is the door shut?"

"It is locked." Julia leaned her forehead against the wood and closed her eyes tightly. How she hated dark spaces, and suddenly the spacious cellar seemed to be closing in on her.

"However did the door become locked?"

Julia shook her head wordlessly.

Marcus banged his fist on the door, shouting, "Hello! Let us out! We're trapped in here."

Julia winced at the word "trapped." "There's no one there. They can't hear us."

"How do you know that?"

"I just know."

"Then we will just have to wait for them to come back. Surely we will be missed before the guests start to arrive."

Julia shook her head again, her eyes still closed.

Then Marcus really *looked* at her, for the first time since the door slammed shut. She was white as snow in the candlelight, and her slender shoulders were trembling. Her shawl lay in a puddle at her feet.

"Julia?" he said quietly. "Are you quite all right?"

"I-I just do not like dark spaces," she whispered. "I don't like feeling trapped."

"Of course not. Here, you should sit down." Marcus placed his candle on a small stone ledge carved in the wall and put his arm around Julia's shoulders. He led her over to sit down on an upturned crate and removed his coat to place it carefully over her thin dress.

"You are wearing the scarab," he said, forcing a light tone into his voice. "That should bring us good luck and get us out of here very soon."

A ghost of a smile whispered over her lips. "I certainly hope so."

Marcus sat down on another crate and took her hands in his, trying to rub some warmth back into them. He decided to distract her with some conversation. "Who is Abelard?"

She looked at him, startled. "Where did you hear of Abelard?"

"You shouted for him just now, when the door shut."

She looked down again, to where their hands were clasped together. "He is the butler."

"I thought his name was Douglas."

"Abelard is his first name."

Marcus was shocked. "You call the butler by his first name?"

She shrugged. "It is a long story."

"It appears we are not going anyplace for a while. Would you like to share the story with me over a bottle of wine?"

"Wine?"

"Yes. There is plenty of it here." He gestured toward the long rows of shelves. "Or perhaps you would prefer sherry or brandy? There is plenty of that, as well. It would help warm you."

"Are you sure it is a good idea to have wine to drink so soon before the ball?"

"It's not as if we're going to become thoroughly disguised or anything like that. Just a little warming sip."

Julia considered this. A bit of wine *would* help to get through this confinement. "Very well. Just a sip."

Marcus disappeared between some of the shelves. There was a loud popping noise, and then he reappeared with a bottle of wine raggedly uncorked.

"I apologize if there are bits of cork floating in the wine," he said, handing her the bottle. "I had to open it with my stickpin." He held up the emerald-headed pin, now hopelessly bent.

Julia laughed. The first drink of wine was already helping her to relax, its warmth spreading to her very fingertips and toes. "It was very good of you to sacrifice it to the cause of wine, Marcus."

"Indeed it was." He took the bottle back from her and drank from where her lips had just been. "Now, tell me the story of why you call the butler by his first name."

Julia took another drink of the wine and said, "Well, you did guess part of the truth the other day. He was once an actor, but he had"—she thought quickly—"stage fright. Terrible, crippling stage fright. He had nowhere else to go, and we had just lost our butler. So my mother let him stay here." She hated to lie to Marcus, but the thought of her friends being homeless held her back.

Marcus seemed to believe that. He nodded and reached again for the bottle. He looked pensively around the dark cellar as he drank. "I haven't been down here in years. I used to play pirates in here as a child."

"Pirates? In the cellar?"

"Yes. My mother never came down here, you see, so she could not scold me for getting my clothes dirty or being noisy. It was a perfect place to hide treasure, as well."

Julia took another drink. "Were you scolded often, then, Marcus?" She gave a little hiccup, but hid it quickly with her hand.

"Not all that often. I learned very quickly how to hide my mischief from my mother, and my father was often away from home." Marcus took a long, thoughtful drink. "The worst scolding I ever received was for sliding down the banister of the grand staircase."

Julia giggled. "*You* slid down the banister, too? I am shocked, Marcus. Shocked."

"Oh, yes. But only once. Mother caught me and spent hours lecturing me on how, as a viscount and future earl, I had certain standards to uphold. A certain example of propriety to set."

"So you never slid down the banister again?"

"Never."

Somehow that struck Julia as being terribly sad.

She took another drink of wine. "Oh, poor, poor Marcus. Missing out on all that fun. You should go and slide down the banister. Tonight. Now. Well, now when we get out of here."

Julia's feet felt hot. She kicked off her kid dancing slippers and leaned back against the wall. All of her fear of being trapped had faded away, and she felt only a giddy well-being. Why should that be, she wondered?

She lifted the bottle for another drink.

Marcus shook his head and took the bottle back for his own drink. "I could not do that. I'm the earl now. I have an example to set. My life is not my own."

Somehow "is" came out sounding like "ish," and that struck them both as being very funny indeed.

"What do you think, that Lady Jersey is going to come from London, see you, and refuse to let you into Almack's the next time you are in Town?" Julia said between her hiccups of laughter. "You can do whatever you like in the privacy of your own home. Or else what use is there in being an earl?"

That made a great deal of sense to Marcus. He nodded solemnly. "You are right. Absolutely. I will slide down the banister this very night."

"Excellent! I will toast to that." Julia tipped the bottle. "It is empty."

"How terrible."

"Yes, indeed. Do you think your pin could open another bottle?"

"I think maybe it could." Marcus stood up to go fetch another bottle of wine and found that his legs were distinctly unsteady. Things were also a bit hazy around the edges.

Surely he had not had *that* much to drink! Had he?

"Does it feel a bit warm in here to you, Julia?" he asked, sitting back down on his crate.

"Um, yes, quite. Perhaps you should take off your coat." Then Julia giggled. "Oh! *I* am wearing your coat."

"Then you should give it back to me so I can take it off."

"Of course. Excellent idea."

Julia stood, wobbling just a bit on her stockinged feet, and went to wrap his coat around his shoulders. As she leaned close, he smelled her sweet lavender scent and felt the brush of her hair against his cheek. Long curls of it had escaped its ribbons and pins.

If he tilted his head just so, he could rest his head on her creamy shoulder. Or he could reach out his finger and trace the interesting pattern of freckles spread across her collarbone.

He *did* reach out and touch the largest freckle, a golden dot just where the graceful curve of her neck met her shoulder. He could not seem to stop himself.

"You are so beautiful, Julia," he whispered, tugging her down so that she sat across his lap. "So beautiful."

She curled against him, winding her arms about his neck. "So are you, Marcus."

"I want to kiss you."

"Then what is stopping you?"

Marcus had just lowered his head to hers, their lips barely brushing, when the cellar door was flung open and a flood of lamplight fell across them.

Standing there were Abelard, Mary, Ned, Lady Edgemere, and Mr. Whitig, all starting in varying degrees of shock.

Julia gave a small shriek and went tumbling off of Marcus's lap onto the floor. Marcus quickly helped her to her feet and stepped in front of her, blocking her from the view of the others.

The wine fumes cleared suddenly from his head.

"We were trapped in here," he said. "The door stuck, and we could not get out."

Lady Edgemere's sharp gaze took in the mess on the floor, the empty wine bottle, and Marcus's coat and Julia's shawl, all tangled up together.

Then she looked up at the disheveled couple.

"So I see," she said. "Well, my dears, I think we all know what this means."

"A wedding. By special license," Mr. Whitig answered sternly.

Julia closed her eyes and groaned deeply, longing to bang her head against the stone wall. Then she opened her eyes and looked straight at the culprits— Mary, Abelard, and Ned. They were trying, without much success, to hide their satisfied smirks.

Julia was absolutely going to kill them.

"Here, my dear. Drink this."

Julia took the glass of soda water Lady Edgemere offered and sipped at it gratefully while she watched the dancers swirl around the ballroom. She had already greeted all the guests, and her cheeks felt frozen in a smile. Her temples throbbed.

Surely they could all read the disaster on her face?

But in reality, no one seemed to notice. They were all much too excited to be in Rosemount's grand ballroom again.

Julia was just grateful that Mr. Whitig had left, taking Mr. Elliott with him. She couldn't face their disapproval just yet.

She finished off the soda water and felt a bit better. Her headache was lessening. "Thank you, Lady Edgemere," she said. "You are so kind."

"Pish!" Lady Edgemere answered, reaching up to straighten her bright green-and-gold turban. "I have often overindulged, myself, and I know how it feels. Is the soda settling your stomach?"

"Yes, thank you." As Julia placed the empty glass on a passing footman's tray, her gaze fell on Marcus. He stood across the room, talking to Lady Angela. His smile looked as frozen and pained as Julia's head felt, as Lady Angela frowned up at him. Lady Angela's slipper tapped, fluttering the hem of her pink satin gown.

Finally, Lady Angela accepted the arm of one of her faithful swains, who led her into the dance. Marcus moved away, out of Julia's sight.

"Lady Edgemere," Julia said softly, "you will not tell anyone what you saw in the wine cellar, will you?"

"Me, my dear? Of course not. I am no tittle-tattle—not about my friends, anyway. But you must know that my silence can only buy you perhaps this evening. Mr. Whitig will have it spread far and wide by tomorrow."

Julia groaned and brought her white lace fan up to hide her face.

"Oh, Julia, it is not so horrible as all that!" Lady Edgemere said with a laugh. "Marcus is an honorable boy. He will do the right thing by you."

"That is what I am afraid of," Julia muttered.

"Whatever do you mean, dear? You are fond of Marcus, I can tell. You will be so much better for him than . . . well, than anyone else ever could be. Your mother and Gerald would have been so happy to see their children settled together. Where is the rub? Everything has worked out perfectly."

Julia just shook her head. How could she explain to Lady Edgemere what she did not even fully understand herself? She did want to marry Marcus. But only if he wanted to marry her every bit as much in return.

Chapter Sixteen

If thou remember'st not the slightest folly
That ever love did make thee run into,
Thous hast not lov'd.

—*As You Like It*

Julia awoke the next morning with a terrible head-ache. It felt as if an orchestra composed entirely of drummers were playing inside her brain. She tried to open her eyes, but the thin line of sunlight peeping beneath the draperies caused a pierce of pain, so she slid back down beneath the bedclothes.

Why did she feel so wretched this morning?

Then she remembered. The wine cellar, the dark-ness, the old fear of closed spaces coming back upon her. The wine, Marcus, their near kiss.

And Lady Edgemere and Mr. Whitig staring at them with shocked eyes.

Julia groaned and buried her head in the pillow, trying to blot out those images.

It did not work. There they still were, flashing end-lessly across her mind. Especially the part about get-ting caught.

She had really landed in the scandal broth now. Before, people had only thought her a bit unusual. Now they would think she was a complete wanton. Mr. Whitig was sure to spread the news, and, if he did not, his wife would. He was a good person, of course, and an excellent steward of St. Anne's, but he was also a terrible gossip. He just couldn't seem to help himself. And one word said "in confidence" to his wife or to a lady in his choir or altar society, would soon spread to the whole neighborhood.

This was surely the most interesting *on dit* the neighborhood had seen since Lord Hallsby's youngest daughter eloped with the music master two years ago. News of Julia's disgraceful behavior would spread like wildfire through the drawing rooms.

Marcus would do the honorable thing, of course. It was the only thing he *could* do, being such an honorable man. He would ask her to marry him, and she would be expected to say yes.

She did want to marry him. More than she had ever wanted anything in her life. She wanted to make a life here at Rosemount with him and raise their children here. She wanted to sit with him before the fire every evening, go to parties with him and talk about them with him in the carriage after. She wanted to breakfast with him every morning. She wanted to travel with him to all the places he had seen. And yes, she wanted very much to sleep with him in the grand bed in the Earl's Chamber every night.

She wanted to be old with him, to shout her conversation into his ear trumpet, and watch their grandchildren push his bath chair around the Pump Room in Bath when they went there to take the waters for their rheumatism.

She longed for all these things and so much more.

She should be dancing for joy that now they would have to be wed.

All she felt was misery. The life she envisioned, the life she longed for, could only be if Marcus loved her and wanted that life in return. If he did not, it would only be a mockery of her dreams.

Surely he would come to resent her, and she would have to watch him take a mistress and drift farther and farther away from their life together. It would be preferable to never see him again than to live apart from him beneath the same roof.

Elly came into the room then, Julia's tray of toast and chocolate in her hands. She helped Julia sit up against the pillows, propped the tray against her knees, and went to open the curtains at the window.

The rush of late-morning light hurt Julia's eyes, but she determinedly went about buttering her toast. She was going to need sustenance for the long day ahead.

"Shall I lay out your blue morning dress, Miss Barclay?" Elly asked, opening up the wardrobe.

"Mm-hmm," Julia murmured around her bite of toast. "Whatever you think, Elly."

Elly nodded decisively. "The blue. You'll want to look your best today, miss."

"Will I? Why is that?"

"Because his lordship has asked if you'll walk with him in the garden, miss. When you're ready."

Marcus paced impatiently around the perimeter of the small summerhouse and took out his watch to check the time again. Where *was* she?

By Jove, but he wanted to get this proposing busi-

ness out of the way so that they could get on with
what was really important. Deciding how they were
going to go on for the next thirty or forty years.

Thirty or forty years.

Marcus ceased his pacing as the enormity of this
situation struck him anew. He would soon be married. To Julia.

A strange new excitement fluttered inside of him.

This was not what he had planned at all, of course.
He had planned to take a Society wife, to resume his
place among the *ton*, and increase the consequence
of the earldom. All of the things he had thought were
so important in his long-ago youth.

But he had found, as he lay awake in the gray-
pink of dawn, that he could let go of those plans
with hardly a pang. Much to his surprise, the thought
of having Julia as his wife was so much more
appealing.

She might have no position of consequence in Society, and her only dowry was that of money settled
on her by his own father. But life with her would
never, ever be dull.

Then he saw her coming along the lavender-lined
pathway to the summerhouse. She wore a very pretty
pale blue muslin dress and a wide-brimmed straw
hat, but her steps were slow and dragging. As she
came closer, he saw that she was very pale, her eyes
wide and anxious.

Not at all like an eager bride-to-be.

Marcus frowned.

Julia looked up, saw his scowl, and turned even
whiter.

Marcus made a concerted effort to smooth his features into unthreatening blandness. He held out his hand to help her up the summerhouse steps.

"I am so glad you agreed to meet me, Julia," he said.

She sat down on one of the benches and removed her hat. Curls sprang free from their confining blue ribbon. "Did I really have a choice?" she murmured in a small voice.

Marcus felt another frown tugging at his mouth again. She was behaving rather oddly, not like her usual ebullient self, and not at all like a woman about to become betrothed to an earl.

"I suppose not," he answered. "Neither of us has the luxury of choice in this matter."

She looked at him, the merest flash of hazel eyes, then dropped her gaze back to the hat in her lap. "And what is this matter?"

"What happened last night, of course! Surely you have not forgotten."

"No. I have not."

"Lady Edgemere and Mr. Whitig came upon us in a rather . . . compromising situation."

"I particularly remember that part."

"Julia, you yourself said that Mr. Whitig is one of the worst gossips in the county."

Julia plucked at the ribbon roses on her hat. "That is true. The poor man just cannot seem to help himself."

"The only way to avert a great scandal is to wed. I *have* to marry you," Marcus said impatiently, puzzled by her distant air. She didn't seem concerned about their situation at all; instead, she seemed very far away. "Therefore, I have the honor of requesting your hand in marriage."

"When you put it so romantically, how can a girl refuse?" she said quietly. "But I fear I must."

Marcus was shocked. He stared openmouthed at Julia's composed face. "Are you refusing me?"

"I am. I am very aware of the great honor you do me, Marcus, but I must decline. I cannot marry you."

He had never been so flummoxed in his life. He had thought the proposal a mere formality before Julia fell on him with grateful kisses. Now she had refused him! He had no idea what to do next.

"You *have* to marry me!" he said, sounding even to his own ears like a petulant schoolboy. "Otherwise there will be a scandal."

"I am used to scandal," she said, her even voice breaking a bit for the first time. "How can I marry you, Marcus? You do not love me."

Love? "You don't love me, either. Marriage has nothing to do with love."

"No. It has to do with land, money, and family connections. I have none of those things. You would do so much better to wed Lady Angela, as you had planned."

Perhaps he *had* thought of marrying Angela, very briefly. But those plans had immediately fallen aside, with nary a qualm, when he decided to marry Julia.

But Julia did not want to marry him. Did she find him so repulsive, then? Was the thought of a life with him complete anathema to her? It had not seemed so, from the sweetness of her kisses.

Marcus was thoroughly confused.

"I did not compromise Lady Angela," he said, raking his fingers through his carefully arranged hair. "I compromised *you*."

"Yes. And you have done the proper thing by offering for me." Julia stood up and came to his side, laying her hand briefly on his shoulder. "That was very dear of you. But I care about you too much to ruin your life. The scandal will only be a nine days' wonder for you, and then you can make your offer to Lady Angela."

She went up on tiptoe and kissed his cheek. Then she smiled and left him. Soon, she disappeared back into the house, and he was alone.

He sank down onto the bench she had vacated, his early morning headache returning a hundredfold. She *cared* about him, but she would not wed him?

What he wouldn't give to know, just this once, what was going on in the labyrinth of Julia Barclay's mind.

"My lord? I am sorry to disturb you, but there is someone to see you in the library."

Marcus sat up, startled. He must have dozed off there in the summerhouse. The shadows were long on the leaf-strewn floor, and one of the maids stood before him, wringing her hands in her apron. She was not one of those odd, winking housemaids; he thought she might be Julia's lady's maid.

"Yes?" he said, still rather groggy. The puzzle of Julia and her refusal must have proved too much for his tired mind. "Who is it?"

The maid bit her lip uncertainly. "Well, my lord, it is Mr. Thompson. Who used to be butler here."

The former butler? What could he want? "I will be in shortly."

Marcus vaguely remembered the man who waited in the library furtively scanning the bookshelves. He had only been the butler for a very brief while before Marcus left, but it was hard to forget those distinctive, rabbitlike features.

"You wanted to see me?" Marcus said, going to stand behind his desk.

The man swung around from the bookshelf, startled. "L-Lord Ellston. I daresay you do not remember me, but I am Thompson, former butler here."

"I remember you. Why have you returned to Rosemount?" Marcus studied the man. He did not like the desperate glow in Thompson's eyes at all.

"I came to retrieve a possession I inadvertently left behind, my lord."

"A book, perhaps?"

"Why, yes, my lord! How did you know?"

"A lucky guess. But how did your book come to be here in the library?"

"I-I am not sure, my lord. Sometimes the housemaids can be very careless."

"Indeed. Well, Thompson, feel free to look about."

"Thank you, my lord." Thompson climbed up on one of the stepladders and began to dig about behind a row of Greek classics. As he did this, he said, "I also find that I can give you some valuable information about your staff, my lord. Something you may not be aware of."

Marcus raised his brow. "Oh?"

"Yes, my lord." Thompson came down from the ladder, a black leather-covered book clutched in his hands. When he turned to face Marcus, his watery eyes gleamed with a certain satisfied malice. "Did you know that your butler is Abelard Douglas, the actor?"

"I know that he is an out-of-work actor whom the late countess took pity on." Marcus looked at Thompson warily. The man sounded rather unbalanced.

Thompson laughed wildly. "He is hardly out of work, my lord! He and his troupe have been here since April, rehearsing for their tour. Or so they said."

Marcus frowned. "Is that so?"

"Yes. And those two footmen I noticed in the foyer are also actors in that troupe, my lord. As is the odd man in the Chinese hat I saw in the garden."

Marcus stared at the man, a dawning realization creeping through his mind.

Thompson might be unbalanced, but what he said made perfect sense when laid against what Marcus himself had observed in the last few weeks. The fact that the footmen dressed so eccentrically, played dice on the floor of the foyer, and spilled syllabub all over guests. The way the housemaids loitered about in the corridors, whispering together, winking and giggling.

They weren't servants at all, they were *actors*. Friends of his father's wife, no doubt.

What a fool he had been.

Julia had thought to hide them beneath his very nose, to make him pay for their upkeep under false pretenses. She had lied to him from the very moment he entered the house.

She had refused his proposal, *and* she had lied to him.

Anger swept through his heart, replacing all the excitement and confusion he had felt earlier.

Thompson slowly approached the desk, still clutching at his book, seemingly emboldened by Marcus's dumbfounded reaction. "My lord," he said, "if this information has any, er, value to you . . ."

Was the little rabbit daring to ask him for money? Marcus shot him a cold glare, and Thompson retreated.

"You have retrieved your property," he said. "If there is nothing else, you may take your leave."

"O-of course, my lord. Good day, my lord."

Thompson beat a hasty retreat, the door to the library banging shut behind him.

Marcus drummed his fingertips on the desk, his mind seething. It was time, past time, for him to have a long-overdue discussion with Miss Julia Barclay.

Julia was coming down the stairs when she saw Thompson crossing the foyer to the front door. She wondered what he could possibly be doing at Rosemount; then she saw the book he was clutching against him. It was the black volume of naughty drawings Daphne had found hidden behind the Plato.

So it *was* his. Julia couldn't help but smile at the vision of the rabbity little man eagerly devouring the drawings.

He looked up and saw her there smiling. His watery eyes narrowed as he shot her a glance filled with venom.

She fell back a step.

"You will not be smiling for long, *Miss Barclay*," he hissed. "Your game is up."

Julia tilted up her chin and said coolly, "I have no idea what you are talking about Thompson. Or indeed why you are here. Did you not resign your position?"

"I worked here for your mother, that *actress*, for four years because my wife enjoyed the niceties of living at Rosemount. If it weren't for your *friends* we would still be here."

"You chose to leave."

Thompson shook his head violently, the book trembling in his hands. "You'll be sorry now. His lordship knows what you've been up to."

A cold knot of ice grew in Julia's belly. "What do you mean?"

"I told him who all your so-called servants really are. That they are your theatrical friends, no better than gypsies, and that he has been duped into paying for their upkeep." Thompson gave a bark of humorless laughter and departed, leaving an echoing silence behind him.

Julia barely had time to process this revelation when Marcus emerged from the library. He looked up and saw her standing there on the stairs.

For one instant, Julia felt she was fifteen again, huddled on the staircase, listening to the quarrel in the library. She took one look at the dark expression on Marcus's face and turned around and ran.

She raced down the corridor into her own room. Before she could shut the door, he was there behind her. Filling the doorway, filling the whole room, with his thunderous presence.

Julia had never seen him scowl like that before, and she did not like it one bit. She tried to cross her arms, to face him with bravado, but her legs felt so weak she had to lean against the bedpost instead.

"You . . . you should not be in my bedroom," she managed to say, inanely. "It is not at all proper."

"Julia," he said, his voice very quiet. "We are so thoroughly compromised that I hardly think my being in your bedroom is going to make a whit of difference. I want you to tell me about the servants."

"The servants?"

"I want the truth. You told me that the butler was an out-of-work actor with stage fright. That is not so, is it?"

Julia knew when she was defeated. She sat down on the end of the bed and said, "No. Abelard is not out of work. He and his troupe are about to embark on a tour, where they are to perform a program of Shakespeare's comedies."

"And the other servants are members of that troupe?"

"Not all of them."

"Which ones?"

"I don't see how that . . ."

"Which ones! Tell me, Julia. Is the cook an actress?" He didn't raise his voice, but his quiet tones rang with authority.

"No, not the cook. Mary and Daphne, the housemaids. And Ned and John, the footmen who wear Renaissance garb. Agnes, whom you have not met. I told you she was my cousin, who is staying here because she is ill. But she is not. That is, she *is* ill, but she is not my cousin. Only my friend." Julia knew she was rambling, but she couldn't seem to stop. If only he would stop looking at her!

"Is that all?"

"There is Charlie. He was digging up the bulbs in the garden. And a young apprentice, who is the bootblack boy. That is all, I promise! All the other servants are genuine."

Marcus sat down slowly on her dressing table bench, his great height dwarfing the satin cushion. The thunder on his face had faded, but now he looked disappointed and sad.

That was infinitely worse than anger.

"You lied to me, Julia," he said softly.

Julia twisted her hands together in consternation. "I know, and I am truly sorry for it, Marcus. I hated it, but I had to protect my friends. They have no money until they are paid for their first engagement, and no place to stay. I couldn't let them be thrown out. This was the only plan I could come up with on such short notice."

"I would not have thrown out any friend of yours. You could have come to me, told me the truth."

"I know that now." After their tipsy confidences in the cellar, she knew it very well. "I know *you* now. But at the time, I was frightened."

"Frightened of me? For heaven's sake, why?"

"You do not know this, but on the day you left Rosemount four years ago, I heard your quarrel with Gerald."

He looked up at her with haunted eyes. "You heard that?"

"I was sitting on the stairs, and you had not closed the library door all the way. You were so angry, so contemptuous of my mother, the *actress*. That was my only memory of you when you returned; how could I trust you?"

Marcus shook his head sadly. "I have bitterly regretted that scene for all these years; I will regret it for the rest of my life." He came to her and laid his palm quietly against her cheek. "Please, Julia. Don't let me regret you as well. Let me do the right thing and marry you."

Julia leaned against his hand for just an instant. "I will never let you regret me, Marcus."

He nodded, then turned around and left. The door clicked ever so softly behind him.

Julia sat there alone for a very long time, crying silently into her hands. Love and remorse and regret sat bitterly on her heart, and she wept for all her foolish dreams.

Then she dried her eyes. "I will *not* let you regret me, my love," she repeated in a fierce whisper. "I will not be the ruination of your life."

There was only one thing she could do.

She went to her wardrobe, pulled out her battered old trunk, a veteran of all the tours she had been on with her mother, and began to pack.

"Where is Miss Barclay?" Marcus asked the unfamiliar footman. The actors were, not surprisingly, not in evidence in the dining room that evening. "Does she not know that supper was meant to begin fifteen minutes ago?"

He looked down the table at Julia's empty chair. He had hoped that once they sat down to supper, once things were in their familiar pattern again, they could begin to talk. He could reassure her, convince her of the wisdom, the necessity, of their marriage. He could make her smile again.

But he could do none of those things if she wasn't there!

"Well?" he asked the footman.

The young man shifted nervously on his feet, his shoulders twitching in his plain black livery.

Marcus rather missed the colorful doublets of Ned and John.

"Did you not know, my lord?" the footman eventually said.

"Know what?"

"Miss Barclay is gone, my lord. She left above three hours ago, with all her actor friends. She told the cook she was going on tour with them."

"What!" Marcus leaped up from his chair, sending the fragile wood clattering to the floor. "Why was I not told this?"

"We thought you knew, my lord. They packed up and left in ever such a hurry."

Marcus ran out of the dining room and up the stairs to Julia's chamber. Surely the footman was mistaken. Surely Julia was just in her room, reading her damnable Shakespeare.

But he found just what he had feared to find in her room. Nothing.

The silver-backed brushes and enameled scent bottles were gone from the dressing table. The doors to the wardrobe hung open, revealing the empty space inside. Even the little French gilt card table that had sat beside the window had been taken.

He moved slowly into the quiet, still room, his steps shuffling like those of a very old man. His shoe caught on an object on the floor, the turquoise-colored silk shawl she had worn to the ball. It had obviously been lost in her hurry to pack and be gone.

Marcus picked it up and buried his nose in the soft cloth.

It smelled like lavender, vaguely like the wine that had been their downfall, and like the elusive sunshine scent that was Julia's alone.

For the first time in many years, since the night he had quarreled with his father and left Rosemount, Marcus cried.

"Julia," he sobbed. "Julia, come back to me. I need you so very much."

But there was no one there to hear him.

"I must say that, even though I am eager to work again, I am very sorry to leave Rosemount." Mary sighed, leaning back against the worn leather cushions of Abelard's lumbering old coach. "It was great fun to be a housemaid for a while."

"*I* am not sorry to leave dusting behind," Daphne answered.

"I only hope we'll be able to find lodgings once we reach Brighton," said Agnes. Her foot was propped between two cushions on Daphne's lap, and she looked distinctly uncomfortable.

Julia tore her gaze away from the window, where

she had been watching the passing countryside in silence ever since they left Rosemount in such a hurry. "Let me pour you some brandy, Agnes," she said, hunting about for the hamper Mrs. Gilbert had packed for them. "You look so pale."

"Thank you, Jule," said Agnes with a small smile. "Brandy would be very nice."

Julia found the silver flask and small cups tucked among the sandwiches and biscuits. She poured out a measure of the amber liquid and passed it across to Agnes. "I am so sorry to be dragging you off across the countryside, Agnes! You should not be traveling."

Agnes shrugged and took a sip of the brandy. "My dear Jule, you must not think of it! You did so much to help us, more than was really humanly possible. We got to stay at Rosemount for much longer than was expected."

"You are a true friend, Julia," said Daphne.

"If only we could have helped you in return!" cried Mary. "We *wanted* to help you, but we only made things worse."

Julia blinked away the sudden prickling of tears. She had been trying so hard to stay calm, to not break down into hysterics at leaving Marcus and Rosemount. Now it all threatened to burst free in the face of her friends' concern.

"You are all the very best friends anyone could ever hope for!" she said hoarsely. "You *do* help me, just by being here." She swept her gloved fingers across her cheeks to wipe away the tears. "I think we should all have some of that brandy."

"What a good idea," said Mary, dashing away tears of her own. She poured out cups for herself, Daphne, and Julia, and passed them about.

"What shall we drink to?" asked Agnes.

"To the future, of course," Julia answered. "And to friendship."

Chapter Seventeen

Play out the play.

—*Henry IV, Part One*

"It's going quite well, isn't it?" Mary leaned over to look in the dressing room mirror, adjusting the frilly fichu over her shoulders. "A full house on opening night is always a good sign."

"And how smoothly the play is proceeding!" said Daphne, twirling her shepherdess's crook. "No one has fluffed their lines at all. Not even John."

Julia listened to their chatter from behind the japanned screen, where she was changing Rosalind's brocade Elizabethan court gown for her Ganymede disguise of doublet and hose. "We have only just finished the first act. We have the rest of the play to go. All of the most difficult scenes are coming up."

"Perhaps," said Mary, touching up her lip rouge. "Still, the applause was quite enthusiastic. And even if the second act is more difficult, it is ever so much more exciting than the first! Just wait until the audience sees Julia in her trousers."

"*That* is what they have all come to see!" Daphne crowed good-naturedly. "Anna Barclay's daughter in trousers. Speaking of which, come out and show us your costume, Julia."

Julia tugged the velvet doublet down a bit further, hoping it covered her backside in the tight hose. How could she ever hope to remember her lines if she was worried about her nether regions showing?

She took one last look in the full-length mirror, straightened her cap on her upswept hair, and stepped out from behind the screen.

"Oh!" cried Daphne. "You look adorable."

"I do not *feel* adorable," Julia growled. "I feel naked."

"Nonsense," said Mary. "You are going to be the toast of Brighton. You'll have your choice of roles!"

"I am only doing this until Agnes is up and about again," Julia reminded them. "Then I am going to buy my cottage, and Anna Barclay's daughter will fade into obscurity once more."

"Well, before you fade away entirely, put on some lip color," said Mary, holding out the pot of rouge.

There was a knock at the door then, and Abelard called, "Are you all dressed?"

"Yes, Abby, come in," answered Mary.

Abelard staggered into the dressing room, his arms filled with a long wooden box. "This just arrived for Julia."

"Oooh, it's probably more flowers!" Mary said. "You are going to need your own hothouse, Julia."

"Maybe it's jewels," suggested Daphne. "Sent by a lovesick admirer."

"It would have to be a case of jewels, in a box that size," said Mary. "Aren't you going to open it, Julia, or are you just going to stare at it? We are perishing with anticipation!"

Julia smiled at her and went to lift the lid off the box. "Never let it be said I allowed my friends to perish from anything. But I don't want jewels, and I don't need any more flowers . . ." Her voice trailed away as she looked into the box.

"What is it?" Daphne asked. Then she, Mary, and Abelard came to peer over Julia's shoulder.

"A lot of stones?" Abelard said, puzzled.

"Who on earth would send stones?" Mary cried. "Is it some sort of joke? Where are the jewels, the roses!"

Julia blinked away a sudden rush of tears.

She reached in and carefully lifted out the object. It was indeed a lot of stones, but they were not just any old stones. They were laid carefully on a painted base, a miniature model of her standing circle.

The circle where she and Marcus had once gone on a magical, full-moon night.

She touched the reproduction of the stone where they had sat together carefully with her fingertip. Her tears were falling in earnest now, splashing off of her doublet sleeve and onto the stones.

How hard she had tried to forget Marcus! She had busied herself with preparing for the play, had worked herself into exhaustion so that maybe, just maybe, she would not dream of him anymore at night. It had almost worked; she had been so tired that all she could think about was putting one foot in front of the other sometimes. She had reassured herself that she had done the right thing by leaving; now Marcus was free to live the life he truly wanted.

Now, looking at the stones, a great wave of homesickness and longing washed over her.

"Don't cry, Julia!" Mary said in dismay. She took out a handkerchief and began blotting at Julia's tears. "You'll muss your makeup."

"Who gave you this, Abby?" Julia cried, swinging around to look at Abelard. "Who sent it?"

Abelard shrugged, bewildered. "I don't know, lass. The stage manager gave it to me and said it was meant for you."

Julia longed to grab the front of his satin doublet and shake him until his teeth rattled. But she would have had to put the model down to do it. "There must have been a card! *Who sent it?*"

"I sent it," a quiet voice said from the doorway.

Four pairs of eyes turned toward the door, and Julia gasped. Marcus stood there, more handsome even than her memories in his black-and-white evening clothes. Tucked in his cravat was a slightly crooked emerald-headed pin.

"I sent it," he repeated. "But I fear I neglected to put a card with it."

Mary, Daphne, and Abelard glanced at each other and rushed for the door, leaving Julia and Marcus alone in the suddenly silent dressing room.

Marcus laid his cloak and walking stick carefully across an empty chair. "I am sorry for startling you," he said. "But you left without saying good-bye, and I had to come and remedy that."

Julia wiped at her eyes with Mary's handkerchief, wishing she had heeded her words about makeup. Surely it was smeared all over her cheeks by now. "What are you doing here? How did you know where to find me?"

"It was not difficult. Apparently, Mr. Douglas

wrote to Lady Edgemere of their tour, telling her the dates and places. She came to me, and told me I was a bloody fool if I did not come after you."

Julia choked. "She said *that*?"

"Those were her exact words. Lady Edgemere, as you know, has always had the tendency to tell the absolute truth, even if it involves cursing like a sailor. And in this case she was quite correct. I know she misses you." He gestured toward the model Julia had placed carefully back on the table. "The stones miss you; no one else has the eyes of the wee ones. And I miss you. Very much."

It was all too splendid to be real. It must be another dream. Julia shook her head. "You feel guilty for compromising me. That is all."

"No! It is not all." Marcus came to her and grasped her arms in a gentle caress. "I love you, Julia."

She gaped up at him, certain she was not hearing right. "You . . . love me?"

"God help me, but I do. Rosemount is much too silent and lonely without you. There was no one to slide down the banisters or go walking in the gardens on a full moon night with."

"Marcus . . ."

"No, Julia, please let me finish. I have been storing up these words for weeks, ever since you left. I *have* been a bloody fool, just as Lady Edgemere said. I've let the expectations of others, of people who don't matter at all, stand in the way of what is truly important. And that is my love for you, and the life we could have together. I know that Rosemount is not nearly as exciting as the theater, but I can take you to other places, too. Italy, Egypt . . ."

"Oh, do shut up, darling!" Julia sobbed happily, throwing her arms about his neck. "I love you, too. You and Rosemount are all I will ever need."

Marcus held her close to him, very tightly, as if she could fly away and be lost to him again. "So you will marry me?"

"You do not only want to marry me because you compromised me?"

"Of course not. Did I not just tell you so? I want to marry you because you, Julia Barclay, are my only love."

"Then yes, I will marry you. Yes, yes, yes!"

"At last!" Marcus kissed her soundly and twirled her off her feet in a big circle. "At last."

But their blissful reunion was soon interrupted. The door banged open and Abelard flew back into the room, his costume crown tilted wildly on his head. "Julia, we have an emergency! You have to . . ." He stopped short when he saw their embrace. "Oh. Please finish what you were doing."

"We *are* finished, Abby." Julia made Marcus put her back on her feet, and she stepped away from him unsteadily. But she kept one hand on his arm, to be absolutely certain he would not suddenly disappear from her. "What seems to be the trouble?"

"That young apprentice has fallen off a piece of scenery, which I *told* him not to climb on, and sprained his ankle! First Agnes, and now this. He is supposed to be in the very next scene."

"Is there no one to replace him?" Julia said, struggling to come down from her joyful cloud and deal with the here and now.

"No one! Unless . . ." Abelard ran a speculative eye over Marcus. "Have you ever thought of giving the theater a try, Lord Ellston?"

Marcus's eyes widened in shock. "No, I . . ."

"What a grand idea!" Julia cried. "We could be on the stage together, dearest."

"I cannot learn lines so quickly," Marcus protested, still stunned at the thought. He, a proper earl, on the stage?

"Oh, you wouldn't have to learn so many lines," Abelard said airily. "You're only going to be playing Corin. A very small part. Ned will help you."

"Please, Marcus." Julia tugged at his arm and looked up at him with beseeching eyes. "It will be such fun. Just this once."

Marcus melted, and the tiny, disapproving voice in the back of his mind faded entirely. "Very well. Just this once. On one condition."

"What is that?"

He leaned closer to her and whispered, "That you wear that costume on our wedding night."

Julia blushed and whispered back, "I have a sword, too. Shall I bring that, as well?"

When Marcus was shoved onto the stage in front of hundreds of staring people, and the stage lamps blinded him, he began to think this was not such a grand idea after all.

It did not help at all that his hose and doublet felt far too small.

Charlie Englehardt, the man Marcus could only

think of as the strange gardener, followed him on-stage and struck an expectant pose. He raised a shaggy brow at Marcus.

Marcus knew he was meant to say something, but he could not for the life of him remember what it was. He wasn't sure he could even recall what his own name was.

Then he glanced back over his shoulder to where Julia waited in the wings. She smiled and nodded, her hazel eyes bright with joyful tears.

Suddenly, all was clear, not only the lines he was meant to speak, but everything else as well. All his life, he had been searching for something, something that eluded him. He had looked for it all over the world, and in Society's and his family's approval.

Now he had found it, in his very own home, with his fairy princess. With her by his side, he knew he needed nothing else.

He turned back to face the audience, and said, " 'And how like you this shepherd's life, Master Touchstone?' "

Epilogue

If it be true that good wine needs no bush,
'tis true that a good play needs no epilogue.
                                    —*As You Like It*

" 'Come little conduct, come, unsavory guide, Thou desperate pilot, now at once on the dashing rocks thy seasick weary bark! Here's to my love. O true apothecary! Thy drugs are quick. Thus with a kiss I die.' "

Ned gulped from his bottle of poison and fell across Daphne, who lay on her bier.

"Is *Romeo and Juliet* really an appropriate play for a wedding celebration?" Marcus whispered to Julia. "It seems rather, well, gloomy."

Julia brushed her lace veil off the shoulder of her white satin gown and whispered back, "Sh! It is very nearly the end. And *Romeo and Juliet* is quite appropriate for any romantic occasion. Since we are leaving for Egypt tomorrow, and probably won't be back for a long while, they wanted to do something special for us."

She patted his arm and turned her attention back to the stage set up in the drawing room. Daphne was stirring on her bier now, while Ned still twitched.

Julia smiled behind her handkerchief. Somehow,

she could not cease smiling, even in the face of the great tragedy onstage.

It had been a most perfect day, indeed. The sun made an appearance, despite the fact that it had rained all the week before, and St. Anne's was filled to the rafters with guests. Lady Edgemere wore a new bonnet of green-and-pink feathers and roses; Mary and Agnes and Daphne looked exquisite in their bridesmaids gowns of blue silk; and Abelard proudly gave the bride away.

Julia did not even cry when Mr. Whitig pronounced the benediction over them. She was far too busy smiling.

But now she tried to look suitably serious as Daphne snatched up Ned's dagger and cried out, " 'O happy dagger! This is thy sheath. There rust and let me die.' "

Then she stabbed herself and fell dramatically across Ned's body.

The audience leaped to their feet, applauding and cheering as the actors came back to life to make their bows.

"Is that the end?" Marcus asked Julia.

"There is usually an epilogue, but Abelard told me they would stop with the deaths. Much more affecting, you know," answered Julia. "So, yes, that is the end."

"Good. Because I have something very special planned for today, myself."

"You do?" Julia said, full of eager anticipation. "What is it? Not more diamonds?" She touched the delicate web of diamonds and pearls that hung at her throat, Marcus's wedding gift to her.

"You'll just have to see for yourself. Come with me, Lady Ellston, my darling wife."

Julia took his outstretched hand and let him lead her out of the drawing room. All the guests followed, eager for Mrs. Gilbert's sumptuous wedding breakfast that was laid out in the dining room.

They all stopped, confused, when Marcus led them not to the feast but into the foyer.

"Marcus! Where are you going?" Julia whispered, every bit as puzzled as the guests when her new husband led her up the stairs. "It is much too early for . . . for *that!*"

Marcus looked back at her and laughed. "My dear, as much as I may wish it otherwise, I know that it is too early for *that*. This is my gift to you."

"Gift! You have already given me too much."

"But this one is the finest of all." They reached the top of the staircase, and Marcus released her hand to hop up on the polished banister. "My gift to you, Julia, is one glorious flight down the banister."

Julia choked on a surprised laugh. "Are you saying? . . ."

"Yes." Marcus patted the length of wood behind him. "Would you care to accompany me?"

Julia looked down the gleaming stretch of the banister into the upturned faces of all their guests. Mary and Daphne had obviously guessed what was going on, and nodded their heads in encouragement.

"Everyone is watching," she murmured.

"That is the best part."

Julia looked back to her husband, to his eager face, and saw what this meant to him. It was not just a childish antic; it was a new freedom, a new beginning.

She grinned at him and unpinned her lace veil from her hair. "You are absolutely right, my dear. Lead on."

Then she hopped up on the banister behind him, wrapped her arms around his waist, and went flying into the future.